To our fathers, Frank Adams and Jim Steffey
who both adored the winter holidays

Two Storytellers and a Magical Bookstore
Bring Fantastic Worlds of Winter Holidays to Life

When Weakness Becomes Power
Arch tries to hide his curse of causing bad luck.
He never imagines his affliction helping others.
But dreadful holiday visitors give him a chance to shine.

The Spark of a Kindred Spirit
Father William Hall loves his tiny Victorian Era London
parish, and helping those truly in need.
But the endless social obligations of securing funding chafe.
Then an offer appears, tempting enough to risk scandal.

When a Disaster Turns into a Dream
Susan works hard to dress up Estonoa for the Santa Train.
Paul looks forward to inspecting the train line every year to
keep Santa on track.
But he jumps at the chance to help rescue Susan's plans.

The Gift of Connection
Mark joins his girlfriend Beth for their first Christmas back
home in the mountains.
Then one gift opens a door neither of them imagined.
What will Mark discover when he steps outside the reality
he's always known?

Finding Family
Alex finally makes the trip to meet his boyfriend's family,
leaving him a mess of joy and nervousness.
Etan worries about first impressions, and longs for Alex and
his parents to fall in love with each other.
Both want to anchor the home they find in each other.

A Tapestry of Holiday Tales:
Winter Adventures from the Odds and Endings Bookstore

Copyright © 2021 by Kari A. Kilgore

All rights reserved

Published 2021 by Spiral Publishing, Ltd.
www.SpiralPublishing.net
St. Paul, Virginia

Book and cover design copyright © 2021 by Spiral Publishing, Ltd.

Cover art copyright © 2021 by frenta | depositphotos.com

ISBN-13: 978-1-63992-012-9
Large Print ISBN-13: 978-1-63992-013-6
Hardcover ISBN-13: 978-1-63992-014-3

Additional copyright information for previously published material at the back of the book.

A TAPESTRY OF HOLIDAY TALES

WINTER ADVENTURES FROM THE ODDS AND
ENDINGS BOOKSTORE

KARI KILGORE

SPIRAL PUBLISHING, LTD.

CONTENTS

INTRODUCTION

For anyone who loves reading or writing, there's an undeniable magic to a great bookstore. The kind you can lose yourself in, much like you do in the pages of a great book.

As far as what *makes* that kind of bookstore, that varies from person to person and even day to day, every bit as much as the definition of a good book does. They can be huge and sprawling, or cozy and intimate. Full of a little bit of everything, or specializing in a certain genre or region.

I think the main thing is you know you're among fellow book lovers when you walk in the door, and you get that wonderful feeling of anticipation.

What new favorite will you discover? Or what long-lost treasure will you bring back into your life to savor anew? Is a new escape or learning experience or passion right around the corner?

Or perhaps a new bookish best friend?

My first trip to the Odds and Endings bookstore—tucked away in my fictional high Appalachian Mountain town of Lightning Gap—started off as a way to capture that magic. I wanted to create the kind of bookstore I'd never want to leave. One that somehow seemed to always have the book I didn't even know I wanted until I saw it.

And sometimes more importantly, the book I truly needed.

Right from the start, I also wanted this to be a fabulous bookstore for writers. In that case, the magic would of course have to include not only everything we could possibly want to read, since reading is one of the most vital functions for writers. It also needed some way to help us capture the most valuable of commodities: time to write.

Even better? A community of passionate readers, ready and eager to support writers in all kinds of fascinating and unexpected ways.

Thus the incredible basement became the main setting, more than the public spaces of the bookstore itself. The true heart of Odds and Endings is hidden away from the casual shopper and reader, and reserved only for the true believers.

A cozy hideaway, stuffed full of one-of-a-kind and beloved books and places to read them? With comfortable chairs and a big, gorgeous fireplace? With an endless supply of tea and coffee, with spirits or without, and delicious snacks?

All that, and you get there through a secret doorway tucked into a bookshelf that only a select few know about?

Oh, yes please!

To make it even more of a dream-come-true situation, the Odds and Endings bookstore has a fabulous writer-in-residence program. So now this lucky writer gets a whole year to live in the bookstore, in a comfortable, private, introvert-friendly apartment down in that book lover's basement.

Sure, there have to be a few public author events and readings, and even those would be all kinds of fun in such a book-crazy little town. But other than that, the writer gets to live in the gorgeous setting of Lightning Gap, surrounded by a fascinating bunch of locals and visitors alike.

I'd created quite a wonderland, but I wasn't quite finished. Because the real magic of this prime residency isn't only for the writer.

Another lucky lover of stories gets to serve as that writer's character. Living out the stories in some way, working as the ultimate collaborator.

Several stories into this fabulous exercise in wish fulfillment, I'm not sure whether I'd want to be the writer or the character in this scenario!

When I settled down to start this holiday collection, I knew I wanted to do something with EllaJane Cole and Chris Ramsey, the current writer/character pair in residence at Odds and Endings. And what could be better than a private storytelling festival of sorts, held in that wonderful basement?

Especially during that odd in-between week for so many of us in the world, when Christmas or Hannukah or other winter holidays have passed, but we're not yet to the new year. Kids are out of school, and many adults have time off as well. Such an odd limbo, and the perfect time to gather with dear friends for storytelling.

Believe it or not, this is where it *really* gets a little strange.

Because I decided EllaJane and Chris would be telling stories set in the worlds of another author, one familiar to the close-knit Odds and Endings family. Another Appalachian author, as a matter of fact, from not all that far away from Lightning Gap depending on how you measure the distance.

Yes, they're telling stories from my own worlds. And I've had an unreasonable amount of fun with the setup for each night of the Mid-Holiday Madness storytelling week, and with writing the stories themselves.

I loved the rather unusual experience of writing fan

fiction with my own worlds and characters, while at the same time watching the story of the two storytellers themselves unfold.

This collection turned into quite the story-in-story adventure for me, and I hope it will for you too!

The first evening gathered around the fire, with suitable beverages and comfy clothing, featured EllaJane and a fantasy tale from my Misfortune and Magic world. Since these stories are epic fantasy set in an alternate world, Arch Knight and his family at Castle Knight don't celebrate our typical holidays. I had a great time with the traditional mid-winter holiday of Hendrefas in the land of Hanferthen, and the challenges of the sort of guests who simply cannot take a hint in *A Timely Bit of the Best Bad Luck*.

Much to my surprise, Chris took his own turn telling the tale on the second night as a blizzard descended on Lightning Gap, reaching into his love of history. *A Meeting of Two Renegade Minds* visits Victorian Era London, and explores the origins of two wonderful characters from my Odd Society series. Father Hall crosses paths with Dr. Jean Marchér for the first time, and neither of them—or a certain scandalized and fascinated corner of London society—will ever be the same.

After a day full of playing in all that snow, EllaJane turned her attention to one of my favorite real-life holiday traditions in the Appalachian Mountains. I took a few liberties with the Santa Train—partly by having it visit my fictional town of Estonoa, Virginia. Susan McFarland has appeared in stories set in another fabulous bookstore there: Clinch River Books. This time around, the wonderful surprise of *The Real Gift of the Santa Train* is all hers.

Chris returns for the fourth night, as he and EllaJane wrestle with a dilemma that seems to be separate from the stories they're telling, at least on the surface. He pays a visit to Hartstown, Virginia, soon to be renamed Bountyfield, and the setting for my Voices Through Time series. Beth Azen and Mark Hersch are celebrating their first magical holiday together in *A Current Made of Joy*, and an amazing surprise waits on their horizon.

The fifth night of Mid-Holiday Madness finds EllaJane venturing into the world of my Storms of Future Past series, with a tale set in Wolf Branch, Virginia. Etan Griffith brings his boyfriend Alex Collins to visit for the first time, and both of them are nervous and excited in equal measures about the trip. The joys of found family end up front and center in *Discovering Home*, as they so often do when I put fingers to keyboard.

As for EllaJane and Chris—and everyone in the Odds and Endings family—they'll definitely be returning. After all, EllaJane's residency is just getting started.

I hope you enjoy getting to know these characters and reading these stories as much as I enjoyed writing them. Each is only a glimpse into a larger world with plenty to explore. You'll find doorways to them all at the back of the book.

I hope you'll want to return and explore more tales. Lightning Gap itself has played host to a variety of genres, with new adventures on the horizon.

You'll discover more fantasy of many kinds at www. KariKilgore.com/Fantasy.

For more visits to the Appalachian Mountains in and around Virginia, head on over to www. KariKilgore.com/TalesfromAppalachia.

If you're in the mood for romance, swing by www. KariKilgore.com/Romance.

You can also check out www.KariKilgore.com to learn more about me and find other short stories, along with novellas, novels, and more collections.

If you want to keep up with what I'm doing next, get free

stories, read exclusive content not available anywhere else, and see adorable pet photos, head over to The Confidential Adventure Club at www.ConfidentialAdventureClub.com. Hope to see you there!

And last but certainly not least, thank you for your support of me and my writing. It means the world to me and keeps me coming back to tell the next tale.

KARI KILGORE

AUTHOR OF THE DREAM THIEF AND FANTASTIC SIDE TRIPS

A Timely Bit of the Best Bad Luck

A MISFORTUNE AND MAGIC STORY

*For everybody who learns to turn a disadvantage
into their superpower*

A TIMELY BIT OF THE BEST
BAD LUCK

EllaJane Cole had spent almost every one of her forty-three holiday seasons in the Appalachian Mountains of Virginia. So she thought she was familiar with all the joy and magic the days between Christmas and New Year's could bring.

A picturesque snowfall more often than not, enough to transform winter-dark and bare trees into a snow globe fantasy land, with the undulating contours of the hillsides underneath only adding dimension and intrigue. Decorations that ranged from the latest in flashy, electronic-modern gadgets all the way to hand-gathered cedar trees and wreaths.

Carefully kept treasures from decades gone by snugged up to brand-new online or dollar store finds.

Her favorites were gleaming glass ornaments of every shape and color, with hollowed out indentations full of elaborate details inside. That or bright, festive scraps of fabric from everyone's sewing piles, stitched up over bundles of hard candies or sometimes leftover herbs and spices after the frenzy of holiday baking. Between those and special-bought oranges, grapefruits, or even tangerines studded with spiky cloves, the heavenly aroma of a holiday house in the mountains alone sent her straight into an intoxicating haze of wintertime nostalgia.

She'd spent a couple of days over in Bountyfield around Christmas this past week, soaking up all that excitement and love with her sprawling, rowdy family. Luckily for her, they'd always been truly the most important and lasting ingredient for holiday delights.

But right now, sitting in her temporary home in the basement of the enchanting Odds and Endings Bookstore in Lightning Gap, Virginia, EllaJane basked in a brand-new variety of holiday magic.

One she was about to add her own unique blend of creativity and excitement to.

She was taking her first-ever turn as the official Odds and Endings Mid-Holiday Madness Bard.

The basement itself set the stage for merriment on a scale she'd hardly dared imagine as a little girl dreaming of telling her own stories someday. Everyone she'd talked to during her first month of her writing residency told her the same thing.

When they first descended the hidden staircase from the main bookstore above, even after thousands of volumes packed all over the huge Victorian house, none of them could take their eyes off all the literary treasures lovingly tucked into every possible space.

Hand-made bookshelves as old as the house lined the walls, all age-worn and dark and beautiful. Each holding everything from ancient and priceless leather-bound books to hardcovers from every era to paperbacks shiny and new or yellowed and often-read. Covering any subject fictional or not, with almost as many reference books as tales sprung from inside a writer's mind.

The only requirement for taking up precious space in the

heart of both the bookstore and the house was that a member of the Odds and Endings family treasured it.

But the truth was EllaJane suspected space in the basement didn't quite work the same way it did out in the world. Time seemed to travel by its own set of changeable rules as well.

All part of the magic of Odds and Endings and Lightning Gap itself.

She'd even found hand-lettered, hand-made paper-and-board books from a century ago, when the house was being built in 1918. Sharing shelf space with scratchy volumes of the history of Lightning Gap, Felten County, and many of the surrounding towns and counties.

With all the different kinds of maps and books of records any writer or book lover or history nerd or map geek could possibly want tucked or rolled or pinned up in between.

Several of those book lovers sat in the basement with her now, relaxed and comfortable in dark brown leather chairs surely nearly as old as the house, gathered close by the gorgeous fireplace. A roaring fire set against a magnificent maple mantlepiece and beautiful hand-painted purple and green tiles drove away the chill of a late December evening.

Much like the distinctive purple house that held the bookstore above, the basement was cheerily decorated for the season. Ropes of sharp-smelling pine and shiny holly, with bright red berries for accents, were draped over every available surface. Very traditional Victorian Christmas crackers—thumb-length cylinders covered with decorated paper twisted at both ends—sat in piles on the mantle and hung from the adorable little cedar tree beside the fireplace.

Underneath the tree, strewn with multicolored versions of artificial candles, stacks of books bound in wide, sparkling green and red ribbons waited for the end of Mid-Holiday Madness. One for each person gathered for this special night.

Not just any books, of course, not at the heart of Odds and Endings. These were collected volumes by several of the authors-in-residence over the years. Most unwrapped, with their vivid covers making up for the lack of holiday paper.

But each bundle also contained secret books wrapped in plain brown paper, carefully chosen for each person, and related to the tales to be told over the next several days. Ella-Jane had helped choose all of them, aside from the one that waited for her.

Any cold that dared linger in limbs or fingers or toes quickly fell victim to a sip of Mrs. Carabelle Seagon's Special Warming Recipe mulled cider, full of cinnamon and ginger and cloves, and a few secret ingredients she'd never reveal.

The not-so-secret addition that warmed inside and out was a generous splash of fine bourbon for anyone who wanted one, for both the cider and the always-available Earl Grey tea.

Mrs. Seagon wouldn't have cleared five feet tall even if she'd ever worn high heels, and tonight she'd dressed her slender frame more casually than usual. Rather than a sensible skirt or sturdy pants, she wore a modern and entirely typical vacation wardrobe of sweatpants and a matching hoodie.

In the same shade of purple as the house, of course, and decorated with sparkling patterns of candy canes in copper and gold.

Her husband Arthur sat in the chair beside her, as always, dressed in a matching outfit in his preferred shade of warm chocolate brown. Everyone else, EllaJane included, had taken on a similarly at-home variety of cozy, loose clothing.

Not a single pair of hard pants anywhere to be seen.

She wasn't quite brave enough to wear her horribly mismatched pajama and robe combination with company there, so she'd opted for charcoal gray sweatpants and her faded Bountyfield High School sweatshirt. No one here had seen her in her eye-straining overnight getup besides Chris Ramsey, sitting beside her on the sofa in his own black sweatpants and t-shirt.

After all, Chris was a vital part of her writer-in-residence year at Odds and Endings. Besides living in his own basement apartment and sharing her night owl tendencies, Chris had played a role in every short story, novella, and novel-in-progress taking shape on EllaJane's laptop.

Not because he was her co-writer, not in the traditional sense.

Chris was more than her muse, too.

Chris was her *character*, and would be throughout the rest of the year of her residency.

And he'd continue to be her storytelling partner over the next several magical nights of celebrating this odd pause between two major holidays, and the restful space before the beginning of a brand new year.

Adorable little antique tables sat between the chairs and sofas, draped with their own evergreen garlands and each sporting a real candle in red, green, silver, gold, or purple, of course. The gleaming wooden surfaces were just big enough to hold the candles and delicate teacups in faintest purple, matching plates stacked high with Mr. Seagon's light-as-air-and-twice-as-crispy ginger cookies, and a book or two.

But none of the six people and one sweet hound dog who'd joined her and Chris for this special evening had any reading material close at hand.

They were here for a different kind of celebration.

When EllaJane and Chris joined in the long, proud tradition of sharing holiday stories told right out loud.

For some reason that no one seemed to remember anymore, but everyone insisted on following for every gathering at Odds and Endings, Mrs. Seagon stood at precisely eleven past the hour, clasping her hands together and sharing an infectious grin.

"Welcome one and all to the annual celebration of the days in-between," she said in her soft, musical voice, her lilting mountain accent bringing a sparkle to every word. "That time of year when all of us who are able take the chance to pause and reflect. To think back on the year getting behind us, and ahead to the new one about to dawn. And most importantly for the Odds and Endings family, the chance to sit back, enjoy each other's company, and take in some of the best holiday storytelling ever to grace anyone's eyes or ears."

Everyone around the circle either applauded or held up their teacups and took a sip, leaving both EllaJane and Chris grinning and blushing at the same time.

Mrs. Seagon sat, and Mr. Seagon stood, holding his own much sturdier coffee mug with the same stylized O&E logo on the side that decorated the covers of the impressive number of books written by other authors-in-residence.

"We have an extra-special treat this year, courtesy of Ella-Jane and Chris. Like any writer worth her salt, and any character, the two of them have been reading up a storm the whole time they've been here. And while like all the rest of us, they love any book that came to life with a little help from Odds and Endings magic, they both happen to have a favorite of all the ones they've discovered on our shelves."

He turned his smiling gaze toward EllaJane and Chris, and she was certain she caught more than the usual mischievous sparkle in his blue eyes.

"That's just one of all the ways these two are *perfectly* suited for each other. Now to avoid spoiling the surprise, I'll let them tell you all about it."

EllaJane blinked, struck by a most uncommon ability to pull words to mind when it came to talking about writing.

And by the stirrings of heat unrelated to either the fire or the bourbon.

She risked a glance at Chris, and his wide eyes were equally dazed. But his slow, shy smile only cranked up her internal fires a little bit more.

None of that changed the fact that six other pairs of eyes were watching her expectantly (the dog was snoring), and the Seagons weren't the only ones with knowing affection in their smiles.

"I... Well, I'll just jump right into the storytelling if that's okay with all of you." She let out a quiet sigh of relief at all the nods and a sprinkling of good-natured laughter. "What we decided is we'll keep the storyteller a secret for now. But I'd bet all of you know at least one of the stories, and we have enthusiastic permission for what we want to do. All I'll say is there are a lot of stories of all lengths, genres, and moods to choose from."

She turned to Chris, thankful that he took up the thread just as they'd discussed earlier that day. That gave her a chance to watch him talk, with a new appreciation for the wavy black hair curling just past his collar, shot through with silvery highlights just like her own, and his lively green eyes.

She decided she was better off ignoring the full curve of his lips right now, and concentrated on his words instead.

"One of the great things about having so many different kinds of stories and worlds to choose from is EllaJane and I have all kinds of room to play and share. So we decided to tell stories about the winter holidays, all set in one of those worlds. These all came to us while we were working together on other projects. And we're both tickled silly to have the chance to share them with you."

He flashed her a confident smile and an encouraging nod. Between that and the bourbon, EllaJane was ready to jump into the story.

"For our first night, we decided to take you to another world altogether. A world of castles and magic and mages, flying horses and monsters and lonely little boys. But with all that, they still celebrate winter holidays together as a family. Even with all the strangeness in the world we're about to visit, I know you'll find a lot you recognize. I hope you enjoy hearing the story as much as Chris and I will enjoy telling it."

EllaJane closed her eyes for a few seconds, letting the crackling warmth and earthy aroma of the fire soothe away her bout of...*curiosity* about Chris.

At least for a little while.

The equally warm expectations of an attentive audience took care of any lingering nerves.

She didn't lose all awareness of him, sitting beside her, sharing his support and lending his imaginative presence in this story as in several others already, with nearly a year's worth ahead of them. She'd definitely have more to consider in that area later.

For now, she opened her eyes, smiled at Chris, and sank into the weird half-trance the two of them shared more and more easily as they learned how to work together.

The *truly* in-between place, where the shared worlds of their imagination—and that of the author who'd brought their borrowed world for the night to life—dwelled and kept their own plans and schemes and secrets.

EllaJane began to tell the tale.

DURING ALL THE days and nights and weeks and months of the year, the secluded reading room was Arch Knight's favorite place inside all of Castle Knight.

Long and narrow, and tucked up against the side of the castle closest to the shelter of the massive peaks of the

Gorowan Mountains, the room was bright and cozy during the day. Light streamed in through several tall windows, but not *direct* sunlight.

Arch's parents and the stern but kind overseers of the Knight family library never tired of reminding him and his brothers and sisters how direct sunlight damaged books, especially the rare and ancient tomes tucked away on the highest shelves.

Arch wasn't sure why they used those books as examples so often, since even with fourteen years and finally starting to grow taller, he was nowhere *near* able to reach them. The special, valuable volumes sat higher than even his father—Lord Moabar Knight—could reach without a ladder.

So those treasures remained safely displayed in all their thick, leather-bound glory on dark wooden shelves set against the gray stone castle walls, with the most valuable and delicate trinkets generations of Knights had brought back from their travels tucked in alongside.

Endlessly tempting and unavailable, even to a curious boy who would never purposely damage a single thing.

Too many things, and animals, and people, and even plants, damaged *themselves* around him for him to ever want to do the job himself.

Several comfortable chairs normally sat scattered around the space, some covered in fabric or soft, rich leather. Most decorated with a colorful wool blanket from his family's herd of Liwith Mountain sheep. Each of the delightful animals held their own shade of red or blue or purple, silver or gold or copper, from their skin all the way out to the fuzziest ends of their wool. They only had their black faces, ears, and hooves in common.

That and their never-ending chorus of fussy *baaaaas* as they ranged around the grounds outside the high gray walls outside the castle, and even more so as they were herded into the protection of their sheep barn inside those walls for the night.

Arch envied his mother Lady Selene getting to work with the sheep, changing into breeches just like he, his brothers, and his father wore. And his siblings for learning the same fascinating trade and many other things forbidden him.

He never meant for anyone or anything to get hurt or broken, and indeed he spent nearly every waking breath doing his best to make sure that didn't happen. To his deep embarrassment and distress, bad things never seemed to happen to *him*.

But no one outside of his immediate family had ever figured out how to turn aside the bad luck that swirled around him like an invisible, ill-tempered cloud.

Thick, multicolored rugs of the same wool covered the stone floors in front of the chairs, made from the twisted tags and discarded ends during shearing time. Arch suspected the mysterious and powerful Honored Mages in distant Dirgelan used the finest Liwith Mountain wool to make their enchanted robes, but no one had ever confirmed or denied the rumor.

Because none of the legendary mages had visited Castle Knight or Fadlonah since years before he was born, he'd never gotten a chance to find out for himself. Assuming he was brave enough to ask such an intimidating woman or man—skilled in ways of magic he'd only read about—such a trivial question.

He himself had breeches and tunics made of that fine and tough wool for special occasions. But he slept under a wonderful blanket made of the knotty discards every night.

Especially this time of year, when fierce mid-winter storms so often kept all of them confined with cold and wind and heaping drifts of snow for long days on end.

That alone was reason enough for the Hendrefas festivals

everyone in the land of Fadlonah and much of the continent of Hanferthen celebrated as the turning of the year drew to a close.

Traveling to each other's homes when conditions permitted, like the last few days had. Staying in and together when moving around was difficult, and venturing out with the equally colorful landhorses was impossible.

Even the magnificent airhorses Arch had only glimpsed on a handful of thrilling occasions, with broad wings and coats more vivid than the sheep, were left helpless in the face of a blizzard screaming down from the Gorowan Mountains.

But anyone who possibly could trade favors or influence for the chance to travel on the great beasts this time of year always did. The easy duty for hardworking airhorses and their riders alone worked as giving thanks for their difficult and often dangerous labor throughout the year. Besides that, the lifting of the traditional prohibition against paying for their services provided a welcome bonus of coin for the riders, along with time to relax.

Not only was ending the year with such an opportunity —covering the same ground in hours that took days on foot —seen as foretelling good fortune for the traveler, but receiving those visitors promised a good year ahead for the generous hosts.

Arch had always heard it said that all the powers that be send those travelers and the good luck, and welcoming them was the only appropriate way to repay such a gift.

Especially if the visitor arrived by surprise, and bearing gifts both unusual and useful, or simply meant to bring delight to all who encountered them.

That tradition normally worked out well for Arch and his family, since they were so far on the edge of the land. Everyone planned for weeks as the season turned toward winter, anticipating Hendrefas visitors. Laying in supplies of strong apple spirit and rich sheep's milk cheese, and preparing smaller versions of the brilliant wool blankets as keepsakes of the season.

A stack of those blankets sat close beside the fire, draped with sparkling red and gold loops of bersaw vines. They grew dark green and prickly during warmer months, to the point that people sometimes used them to scrub gardening tools that had gotten dirty or rusty. But with the first hard freeze, the bersaw transformed itself into feather-soft beauty, lending its spicy and earthy aroma to Hendrafas and the long, cold months that came after.

Arch and his brothers and sisters had contributed to the supply of gifts for potential visitors, sorting through their clothing and possessions for items that no longer fit or had been replaced. They'd all been cleaned or mended, or combined into quilts or new garments, then combined with similar collections from the reading room and the rest of the castle. A variety of glass jars and ceramic holders full of herbs and medicines for the winter agues that too often struck after the holiday waited, courtesy of the castle's healers as they worked to train new helpers.

Despite his normal love of the joyful Hendrafas festivities, Arch knew he wasn't the only one wishing one of the terrifying storms rolling in from the Nifendraw Sea had cut them off from the outside world on this particular night.

Then they wouldn't have had to deal with the most annoying, overbearing, obnoxious visitors in anyone's recent memory, during mid-winter or any other time.

The reading room's long wooden tables—normally reserved for study or quiet games, or gifts for the welcome travelers as the year drew to a close—were now covered with sturdier versions of the models Arch and his sisters and brothers often made of bits of wood and rocks. Sometimes, as they grew older, they'd been allowed to work with his father's set of tiny enchanted blocks that looked, felt, and acted exactly like the stones of Castle Knight itself.

Arch had enjoyed such games by himself, far enough away to allow the others to build without constantly having to start over when their constructions tumbled themselves down for no visible reason at all.

What took up their normally festive table now had been made not by the curious and sometimes clumsy fingers of children. Playing and learning in equal measure, enjoying each other's company in silence or soft conversation.

These had been constructed by skilled artisans in the far away land of Hameatha, halfway across the great continent of Hanferthen. Many weeks journey even with strong horses, or in more hospitable weather.

So the family who'd traveled all that way in the depths of winter never tired of pointing out, along with how much coin the models of their vast residence had cost them. Models they'd brought along on their difficult journey, in hopes of impressing Lord Moabar and Lady Selene Knight enough to agree to an alliance between their two families.

Not an alliance based on trade, which Arch thought might have made sense if approached in a more polite way. After all, Hameatha was home to vast, unimaginable stretches of fertile farmland, far superior to the fields that lay below Castle Knight. And Castle Knight protected a vital trading port on the dangerous Nifendraw Sea, which stretched out in frigid rage to lands neither Arch nor anyone else in all the lands around Castle Knight knew much about.

But an alliance based on those two strengths might have been a reasonable one to discuss, if not brought up at all during the quiet and relaxation of the mid-winter festivals.

Rather than simply being ill-timed, though, the eldest members of the wealthy Nifoes family had ventured into downright rude.

Following the custom of their land (and determined to ignore the customs of Fadlonah and the Knight family), they'd instead proposed negotiating for not one but two of Arch's siblings in marriage. His oldest brother Rick and oldest sister Tessa were the intended targets, and no amount of polite refusals and detailed explanations had so far deterred the Nifoes from their goal.

For their part, Lord and Lady Knight sat at the far end of the table, faces pleasant and strained, no longer pretending interest but not willing to abandon their three oldest children to such a challenging evening. But they'd told Tessa, Rick, and Arch hours ago that it was best to be welcoming and polite, with strong reassurances that no marriage proposals would be allowed.

Sending the travelers back out into the cold night, even travelers who clearly had a very different understanding of the spirit of the Hendrafas festival, would be inhospitable in the extreme.

All three of the Knight children had admitted being jealous of the youngest two being sent away to entertain themselves, and freed from social obligations.

Right now Rick and Tessa sat together on one side of the table, each nodding politely as gray-haired Ansel Nifoe and his wife Dreyen pointed out features too small to see. Each of them wore the coarse woven cotton clothing of their region. Ansel in rather dull brown breeches and tunic, Dreyen in a slightly brighter yellow dress.

Both were likely pleasant enough to spend time with under different circumstances. What had Arch, his parents, and everyone else terribly confused was the fact that they hadn't even brought their own daughter and son along on this mission.

Arch wondered to himself what that said for the potential spouses and their personalities.

From his vantage point several feet away, far enough away from the chest-high stone fireplace to avoid possible disaster, Arch had to admit he understood why Rick and Tessa had drawn the Nifoes' confused and remarkably stubborn attention.

Rick was nearly as tall as their father, and like Arch, had their mother's thick, wavy black hair. Tessa had their father's sandy hair, falling loose and free as any unmarried woman's did, and took on more of Lady Selene's womanly form as each day passed.

Both of them alternately annoyed and frustrated Arch, as sisters and brothers seemed destined to do. But both were also intelligent and kind, and tolerated his outsized need for attention, since making friends of his own was nearly impossible given his affliction.

And they both chose that moment to sip from thick mugs of warm apple cider, and their shoulders rose and fell in unison. Leaving Arch struggling to hold in laughter that wouldn't help anyone, least of all him.

"That's a remarkably sensible design, Dreyen," Tessa said, following the Nifoes' insistence on being called by their given names. "I expect our farmers might want to consider some of those changes before the next harvest season. I'll pass it along to them, and we certainly appreciate you for sharing."

Dreyen shook her head, and Arch could see a mildly disapproving expression cross her face.

"Well of course you wouldn't pass it along to them, Tessa. That would certainly be left to the next *holder* of Castle Knight. Rick would be more interested in handling modifications to what you do here. You would be best suited to helping improve the habits and procedures in your new home. Wherever that turns out to be, I'm quite certain you'll bless them with new joy and life."

This time Arch covered his mouth with one hand,

wondering how both of his strong-willed siblings would respond. Their mother raised her eyebrows, and their father didn't quite manage to conceal his smile.

"I'm afraid that's going to prove another difficulty in your plans," Rick said, his voice taking on a patience Arch couldn't imagine holding within himself. "Tessa intends to hold Castle Knight, you see. And I intend to travel as much as I can manage, in hopes of building new alliances with strong families such as yours."

Both Ansel and Dreyen sat back, with the first signs of frustration clear in their frowns and scowls.

For her part, Tessa only nodded, with a smile no one could fault as being impolite. But one nobody who actually knew her would mistake for happy.

Arch was impressed with her for not storming out of the room, and with Rick for not pointing out that marrying anyone's *daughter* wasn't in his plans at all.

The Nifoes turned toward Selene and Moabar Knight, probably hoping the parents in the room would help their unruly children see reason. And as promised, their parents offered support, if not an escape from the situation.

"This is true," Selene said, with her own calm smile. "Tessa has been working with Moabar for quite some time now, learning the difficult job and responsibility of holding. One he learned from his own mother, Lady Prenema Knight. While Rick will resume his travels with the spring thaw."

Ansen Nifoe pursed his lips, and gave the slightest shake of his head.

Not obvious or noticeable enough to cause offense, certainly. But more than enough to make the intention of his next words clear.

"Such are the fleeting desires and dreams of youth. Both of you will understand the needs and duties of maturity over time. And come to see what will be best for you and your families."

At that inclusion of some undefined other family—surely meant to mean himself and his wife—Tessa slowly turned and focused on Arch. She widened her eyes and stared at him, then mouthed "help" before turning back.

Without thinking of the consequences of his actions for everyone around him—a most unusual experience for him—Arch got to his feet. He smiled at his parents as he slowly walked toward Tessa and Rick, and the Nifoes across from them.

And the terribly expensive model on the table.

A brief start of alarm crossed his mother's face, but only for a quick second. She let out a silent sigh and nodded, as subtle as Ansen's head shake.

Arch's father still smiled, but it deepened to include his blue eyes.

The Nifoes barely glanced his way, then Dreyen pointed to another of several tall, rectangular replicas of grain storage barns on their intricate model. Much larger and higher than anything around Castle Knight or across Fadlonah, to be sure, and not at all suited for the heavy loads of snow common this time of year.

"We use this one to hold any crops that want drying," Dreyen said, pride clear in her voice. "You can see how the walls have openings, here and here, to allow wind to pass through and do much of the work for us."

Before she had a chance to demonstrate, several tiny pieces smaller than Arch's pinky finger fell off the barn, clattering against the table.

Ansen scowled, with no attempt to try and hide it this time.

"I expect the strain of travel weakened the connection there. I assure you, those are meant to turn as they open and close. We don't bother with removing the sides altogether any longer."

He reached toward the barn, surely meaning to retrieve the fallen pieces, but he managed to knock his mug of cider over instead. Rather than falling in the direction of his hand's motion, it spun as it landed.

Sending the sharp aroma of apple into the air, and the dark, slightly fizzy liquid cascading into his wife's lap.

Who promptly tipped her own cider over as she stood, resulting in the mug shattering despite not traveling any distance. The resulting spray of cider and bits of ceramic landed on the model.

Where more than one well-built wall—that couldn't possibly have been knocked loose by such a small attack—collapsed inward.

Leaving the roofs of two of the barns, one of the stables, and the main house tilted at a most unsteady angle.

And Arch was still nowhere near close enough to touch any of it with his hands or even his feet.

But the reach of his condition or curse or whatever it was clearly exceeded his own.

He stepped back as both Nifoes shoved their chairs back and stood, sputtering and red-faced, but thankfully unhurt.

"Oh no," Tessa said, with what sounded like sincere concern in her voice. "Your lovely models! Take care you don't cut yourselves on the broken bits of mug."

Arch's parents both stood as well, and Lord Moabar spoke for the first time in quite a long while.

"I'm certain we can have those repaired for you before you depart in the morning. Our craftspeople may not be the fine artisans you employ in Hameatha, but they keep everything in Castle Knight in good repair despite the rigors of five rowdy children."

He winked at Arch, who grinned and withdrew back to his chair before anything else went amiss.

"That won't be necessary," Dreyen said, busily wiping at the stained yellow fabric of her skirt. "We'll simply return it to those same artisans to put everything to rights. Thankfully I was nearly finished explaining the designs to Tessa and Rick."

Moabar Knight shook his head, and his expression tilted toward stern.

"The truth is our audience this evening has come to an end. We truly appreciate your visit after such a long journey, and our children have enjoyed your fascinating explanations. I certainly hope you'll accept gifts of the bounty we enjoy here in Fadlonah, as we've welcomed the gift and honor of your visit. The hour grows late, though, and our children have made their answers clear. We have and will always respect their decisions in such matters."

Lady Selene stepped forward, her arm linking through Moabar's.

"I'll show you to your rooms so you can take your rest before you leave us. Thank you for a most interesting evening."

She glanced at Arch on the way by, with a bright and relieved smile. When she stopped at the door with one arm raised toward the hallway beyond, even the stubborn Nifoes couldn't refuse. They muttered their goodnights and hurried from the room.

As soon as Selene closed the door behind herself, Tessa and Rick burst into helpless laughter, and even their father grinned.

"*Thank* you, Arch," Rick said between gasps for breath and renewed giggles. "I don't think anything else would have done the job unless we'd picked the whole thing up and chucked it out the window."

Arch stood and bowed low enough to brush his knuckles against the nubby rug at his feet.

"My pleasure, my dear brother. I'll let you know once I decide what my reward from each of you shall be."

Their father picked up one of the fallen shutter pieces and held it up to the light.

"Had you planned that out between you, then? Having Arch come to your rescue?"

Tessa wiped at her eyes and shook her head.

"Not at all. I just…had a feeling he could help us is all. And he certainly did. Otherwise I'm afraid I would have smashed the whole thing myself."

Lord Moabar carefully replaced the bit of wood and smiled.

"I suppose in this case, whatever changed the course of the evening without causing injury or a lingering case of hard feelings was a wise decision. I wouldn't dare try to pack this back up for fear of breaking something else through an *honest* accident. But the least we can do is mop up the cider before we all retire for the night. We'll gather for a much more pleasant celebration tomorrow evening."

Arch kept himself well back as his father, Rick, and Tessa gathered up enough cloth napkins from a stack left at the start of the evening to blot away the spills. Neither he nor anyone else understood why, but he could generally play games by himself or with someone in his family without results this dramatic.

But he'd done more than enough tonight without risking damage to more of the Nifoes' treasured model. The damage to their egos from being turned down by not one but both of their intended marriage targets would surely be enough to deal with on the long journey back down to their plains homeland.

Perhaps they'd encounter another family willing to strike an alliance on their terms along the way.

One of his fears—kept so far in the back of his mind that he was rarely aware of it—was that he'd never have the chance to find a partner of his own when the time came. A fear best not entertained unless or until he was faced with the reality.

For now, on this strange evening during his favorite time of year with his family, he was content to hug each of them on the way out of the reading room.

And to look forward to better days and nights ahead.

As soon as EllaJane stopped speaking and executed a seated bow, everyone in the cozy basement of the Odds and Endings bookstore burst into applause.

She took a few seconds to truly reenter what most called the *real* world as she always did, gradually leaving the stone walls and howling winds of Castle Knight behind. Bringing herself back to a much smaller room equally dedicated to books and reading.

But this one full of comfortable leather chairs and sofas, with the aroma of Mrs. Seagon's wonderful tea and especially fine bourbon in the air. And a fire surrounded by wonderful purple and green tiles rather than gray stone.

She and everyone else wore modern sweatpants instead of wool or cotton, surely easier to keep clean with the convenience of washers and dryers. Even with none of them covered in magically spilled apple cider.

The best anchor of all, one she'd come to rely on over the past few weeks, was looking into Chris's eyes. He grinned back at her and leaned in for a quick hug.

Something else they'd done many times since she'd

surprised him on the stairs a few days after her arrival and nearly sent them both tumbling all the way back down to this basement. But for the first time, EllaJane felt an altogether new and pleasant tingle at his touch.

The look in his eyes and softness to his smile had her thinking he might just feel it too.

"That was simply wonderful, EllaJane and Chris," Mr. Seagon said, sitting forward and rubbing his hands together. "Thank you both so much for starting our storytelling celebration off right. I do have to ask if you'll be sharing the name of your mystery author now, for those of us who might not have read those particular books just yet?"

EllaJane looked around the room, trying to get a sense of who'd guessed and who hadn't.

From the balance of puzzled looks and satisfied smiles, she and Chris had done quite well in choosing their opening tale.

Their absent writer-partner would be delighted to hear it.

"I believe we'll wait a bit longer," she said, and Chris nodded beside her. "You'll just have to come back tomorrow night for a brand-new story set in an entirely different world."

In the good-natured responses, EllaJane turned to Chris again.

"We'll just see what we both dream up," he said loud enough for only her to hear.

KARI KILGORE

AUTHOR OF PROTECTING HER OWN AND THE DREAM THIEF

A Meeting of Two Renegade Minds

AN ODD SOCIETY HOLIDAY STORY

In celebration of friendships
that begin with an instant spark

A MEETING OF TWO
RENEGADE MINDS

CHRIS RAMSEY SAT in the coziest, most welcoming room he could have imagined, in the company of new friends who loved books and stories as much as he did. But all that, expertly made relaxing tea, and a hearty shot of fine bourbon couldn't wash away his nervousness on this special night.

The hidden basement of the Odds and Endings book-store never got all that cold, not even during the strange days between Christmas and New Year's Eve. Not And not even as a howling snowstorm raged outside, effectively cutting off the high mountain town of Lightning Gap, Virginia, from the rest of the world.

But the attendees at the second evening of this year's Odds and Endings Mid-Holiday Madness enjoyed a roaring fire, wonderful company, and the promise of a wonderful holiday story to come.

The basement somehow sprawled much larger than the gorgeous purple Victorian house above it, with more than enough space for several rooms packed full of books trea-sured by the Odds and Endings family. It also held two spacious and comfortable apartments: one for Chris, and one for EllaJane Cole, the writer-in-residence he was lucky enough to be partnered with for the rest of her year.

But none of that oddly large space mattered nearly as much as the circle of comfortable brown leather sofas and chairs gathered around the huge fireplace. Cheery yellow light reflected off the green and purple tiles around it, all hand-painted and installed as the house was built over a hundred years ago.

For this special time of year—the gap between one big holiday and the next, and the waning of the year—the mantle was piled with garlands of holly and pine, and the goofy stockings he and EllaJane had received from the Seagons still hung sweet as could be.

Each was an oversized hand-knitted sock with their names and the Odds and Endings logo in white, and the rest made with what had to be every color wool had ever been dyed. He could pull his almost up to his hip with plenty of room to spare, and it had been stuffed full of fruit and nuts and hard candy in the most amazing variety of shapes and sizes, along with his very own Odds and Endings coffee mug and t-shirt.

He knew he'd hang that stocking wherever he lived and treasure it the rest of his days.

Little antique tables tucked in between the seats held delicate, light-purple teacups, steaming forth the citrusy bergamot of Earl Grey tea or mulled cider for the holidays. No matter what Mrs. Carabelle Seagon—one of the owners of Odds and Endings—served to her guests, she always started with that proven and reliable base.

Tonight Chris detected a more earthy scent, with hints of apple and possibly...cardamom?

He wouldn't dare ask for her secret, any more than he would pry into exactly how old Mrs. Seagon and her husband Arthur actually were. Chris had been visiting this enchanted bookstore in the heights of the Appalachian Mountains for decades, from when he accompanied his Auntie June when he was a kid up until his current age of thirty-eight.

The first time he'd entered The Contest for himself instead of hearing Auntie June talk about it and daydreaming about it. That was how Chris finally got to take his year-long turn as The Character for the writer-in-residence.

In all those years, he'd never seen the Seagons age. Not one little bit. They'd always appeared they way they did right now, once you looked past the unusually casual wardrobe. He would have guessed somewhere in their late sixties, but with curiously unlined faces to go with their diminutive stature and silvery hair.

Right now Carabelle wore an adorable sweatsuit the same purple as the night before, but this one sparkled with silvery outlines of the constellations in the sky. Arthur, in his constant spot in the chair next to hers, wore a dark-blue version with the same nerdy highlights. Both of them sipped their own bourbon-laced tea, beaming at the circle of dear friends around them.

All of them dressed just as comfortably, making it clear this truly was a family.

A family Chris was terribly afraid would be disappointed by the time they went their separate ways this evening. Especially considering what a wonderful job EllaJane had done as storyteller the night before.

Because tonight, Chris was going to step out of his supporting role and onto the metaphorical stage himself.

He'd be the one providing the entertainment, the reflection, the traditional honoring of the quiet days as the year drew down to a close.

And he was certain he'd find out just how much harder it was to be the one telling the tale rather than experiencing it.

He'd given up on trying to participate in the quiet conversation a while ago, when he kept losing the thread. He was terribly afraid that either asking everyone to repeat themselves or saying something that made absolutely no sense would convince everyone he wasn't ready before he even got started.

So he'd settled for listening, as he so often saw EllaJane do when they were out doing research together. She sat beside him on one of the sofas, clearly far more relaxed than she'd been the night before.

Even though her story of a lonely boy in a land of magic and castles using his bad luck for good had been wonderful, she'd admitted to Chris later that she'd been scared to death. Afraid not a single word would make it out of her mouth.

And that if any did, they wouldn't make sense no matter how generous and supportive her listeners tried to be.

Too late, Chris realized thinking about that right now— both her late-night confession and the fact that she trusted him enough to share it—had been a terrible idea.

If the writer-in-residence had been so worried about doing a rotten job, what possible chance did *he* have to pull this off?

He caught EllaJane watching him with a smile, something that he should have been used to after several weeks of working together. Her telling him about what she wanted to write next, him telling her about his daydream or nightdream acting the story out. Living it.

No matter how much he'd heard his Auntie June talk about how much she loved being a character, and the fact that she'd returned to work with her writer again and again, Chris was constantly amazed at how much he loved every second of it.

He was already getting little flashes of dread about the end of his year with EllaJane.

And after last night, when they'd slipped into their story-telling trance together in front of other people for the first time, he'd started to wonder in the back of his mind if there might not be another option.

As was the long-standing tradition at any Odds and Endings gathering, even if no one knew why, at precisely eleven past the hour, Mrs. Seagon stood and tapped the side of her teacup with a delicate silver spoon. All conversation stopped at once, and Chris was a little bit afraid his heart would do the same.

"Welcome one and all to our second night of our Mid-Holiday Madness storytelling. With the snow really piling up out there, I appreciate you all for making the trip." She set her cup down on the table beside her, then turned back with both fists firmly planted on her slender hips, glaring at their guests. "And I certainly hope some of you have made arrangements for staying in town rather than attempting to drive back up the Lightning Rock Road tonight."

All eyes turned toward Venus Mullins and her best friend Ivy Gweddon, sitting on the sofa across from Chris and Ella-Jane (and thankfully taking the attention away from Chris).

Chris had never seen Venus wearing anything he wouldn't call spectacular, and tonight was no exception. Her wide-legged midnight-blue pants and thigh-length tunic had an iridescent shimmer that danced and shifted with the fire-light, and she'd worked some kind of sparkling blue gemstones into the thick silver braid pulled forward over one shoulder.

Like everyone else, she'd left her sturdy snow boots beside the stairway, but her puffy pink socks had a glow entirely on their own.

Ivy on the other hand wore a pair of sturdy brown sweat-pants with a faded green flannel shirt, with her short, steel-gray hair untouched. Her big blue eyes twinkled, though, as she absently scratched the ears of the big red hound dog sprawled between her and Venus. Chris had taken every chance he could get to rub BeeGirl's head and back and belly, soaking up her sweet redbone hound goodness.

"I suppose Venus and me will do just fine, Carabelle," Ivy said in an exaggerated slow drawl. "Assuming we don't drink enough of your bourbon that we can't make it across the street to Kay and Adam's place."

Venus nodded, her jeweled hair throwing sparkles across the thousands of books all over the walls.

"That or the snow doesn't fall so deep we get lost trying to find our way there."

At that, Kay herself, owner of Kay's Café tucked into the ground level of the Victorian house in question, thew up both hands. Her signature strawberry blonde hair still looked as perfectly curled and coifed as it did at work, and she'd added sprigs of holly and mistletoe to liven it up.

But she'd traded in her perky uniform for a sky-blue footie pajama set. Goofy white soles on the feet and everything.

"I imagine we'll just head right back over here if we get lost," she said. "Bunk down with you."

Her husband Adam, the best old-school soda jerk Chris had ever come across, shrugged and pulled his sunshine yellow robe tight.

"We'll be fine. BeeGirl can sniff the way."

Carabelle Seagon held up both hands and took her seat.

"Just as you wish. Now, we have a special treat this evening, one befitting the storm and this wonderful week at the turn of the year. We'll have the unusual pleasure of hearing not from our writer-in-residence, but from her all-important writing partner. Chris, the stage is yours."

Everyone applauded, including EllaJane, her face lit up with a huge, encouraging smile. Even BeeGirl managed to rouse herself from her cold-weather slumber enough to look up, thump her thick tail several times, and flop her head back down.

Chris did his best to ignore the loop-de-loops in his belly.

"Thank you, Mrs. Seagon. I already know I'll never tell a better tale than EllaJane tonight or any other night, so thank goodness that pressure is off. What I've got in mind is a short story from another of our favorite Odds and Endings writer's worlds. Quite a world away from the not-snowbound-enough castle from last night. But I think you'll still find a common thread between the stories, and between where we sit and where we're going."

He paused long enough to take another sip of tea, letting the soothing herbs and the bourbon's spicy fire get his throat ready for the telling. He'd have to rely on his mind—and his increasing connection with EllaJane—to do the rest.

"We're traveling to another time and place, in a distant land with a legendary queen. One you'll recognize, at least on the surface. And much like this queen, we'll meet a woman who is determined to do things her own way. And the unlikely man who's determined to help her do just that."

Chris glanced at EllaJane, once again taking in her smile, and the glow in her cheeks. Something had shifted between them over the last twenty-four hours, adding the heat of curiosity to their close friendship.

Something he hoped to explore later on.

But for now, the tale was his to tell.

He closed his eyes for a second, letting himself slip into the near-trance they shared when they worked together during the day.

Consciously stepping over to the other side of the connection.

And the storyteller opened his eyes.

FATHER WILLIAM HALL fully understood why he had to attend at least a few of the social events of the London season, especially so close to Christmas.

His Catholic parish was one of a precious few in the seat of power for the Anglican Church, with one of the most powerful heads of that church on the throne for decades already in Queen Victoria. So every bit of goodwill and familiarity he could build up would only help him and his causes, personal and church alike.

The wealthiest and most generous Londoners could make a world of difference for the vital charity work he wanted to do, with the city's poor population huge and seeming to grow every day.

The simple dignity of a warm meal and a safe place to eat it could change an out-of-work man's day for the better, and maybe send him through to a better one.

But that simple meal and the means to provide it wouldn't materialize from the eager generosity of Father Hall's heart. And the Church alone didn't seem to understand how deep the need had become, and that it reached far beyond the men struggling for work.

Women and children needed help too, and often even more so.

These moneyed donors could change and save lives, and all for the cost of a few hours of his time.

And still, he was painfully aware of how out of place he was in his black cassock nearly brushing the floor, and his notched white collar perched on top. Everyone else he saw—at least everyone wearing what could fairly be called a dress—was a riotous explosion of color.

Brilliant pinks and blues, yellows and reds. All gleaming

or sparkling, with full skirts swaying and towering hair bobbing to and fro as they talked.

Even the men showed some flashes of color and style compared to himself, with their black tailcoats revealing white shirts underneath and sprigs of greenery tucked into their pockets. The watch chains stretching across their middles were adorned with all manner of trinkets, shining with gold or silver or flashes of colorful gemstones.

The dull roar of conversation in the vast, warm ballroom also left Father Hall feeling exhausted and overwrought. He hadn't sought out the quiet, solitary life of a priest because he enjoyed trying to keep dozens of people's ranks and annual incomes and degrees of influence organized in his mind.

The warm, steamy atmosphere full of countless competing varieties of ladies' perfume mixed in with the piney scent of greenery tucked into and hung from and bunched along the bottom of every possible surface only made everything worse.

Not one but three of the Christmas trees that had come into fashion over the past thirty years since Queen Victoria married Prince Albert and brought his German traditions to England. These were all hung with painted glass ornaments highlighted by candles flickering from their branches.

One long table held a truly dizzying array of Christmas cards and postcards, another new obsession in post-mad London that had taken hold within his lifetime. Father Hall sometimes wondered what the bright illustrations had to do with the season as celebrated by the Church, or the Bible stories his family had always spent their distant countryside Christmas Day reading.

The few cards they'd given or received back then were hand-made by children rather than purchased.

But no part of him could fault the warmth of time spent with family and friends, or the generosity people who threw these overwhelming holiday balls often shared with those in the city who needed it most.

A boy dressed in what looked like a horribly uncomfortable miniature version of the men's tailcoats walked toward Father Hall, tray of strong, fragrant mulled cider and wassail high over his head. A refreshment room off to the side was well-stocked with other libations to go with biscuits and cakes and sandwiches.

Thank heavens this boy had paid attention to Father Hall's request for an ordinary glass of water when he'd first arrived. Mainly because he very much wanted to keep his wits about him in such unfamiliar surroundings.

The lad paused long enough for Father Hall to retrieve the single clear glass among hearty tankards, and to receive a nod and a sad few pennies in return. When he scuttled off, Father Hall worried he'd violated one of the many rules of etiquette he admittedly wasn't familiar with.

But the entry of several men in matching burgundy jackets and powdered wigs, stringed instruments at the ready, let him know his troubles were worse than that.

Music and dancing were soon to begin.

Along with a flurry of mothers with marriage-aged daughters who for some reason decided dancing with someone as exotic as a young Catholic priest would be a lovely addition to their evenings.

He began to inch backward, hoping to retreat to the balcony and the damp chill of the December evening at least long enough for the swirling forms of the first dance to come to an end. Even if he'd wanted to dance, he had no idea how, and no real inclination to learn.

As the band settled into a collection of curved wooden chairs upholstered in gleaming gold right in front of the largest of the Christmas trees, the flurry of movement of young people in the room took on a new urgency. Huge skirts and hair gathering with their own kind, and dark-suited men doing the same.

Only sedate, already paired couples drifted toward the middle, ready to lead the youngsters in the latest social ritual.

Through the rainbow of motion Father Hall caught sight of another black-robed figure without a powdered head. A line of tension across his neck and shoulders relaxed when he realized it was possibly the one person he knew out of the entire crowd.

Bishop Alfred Bassingham oversaw several Anglican churches near Father Hall's modest spiritual home, but he'd taken the time to get to know all the clergy members established in the same neighborhood. He'd also been the one to encourage attending these parties so the patrons wouldn't overlook the rare Catholic Church when they felt the need to atone for their own sins, and their often-staggering prosperity.

Tonight Bishop Bassingham had shed his impressive, colorful vestments and opted for a black cassock similar to Father Hall's. At first glance he seemed rather ordinary without his bright clothing, but only until one caught sight of his lively brown eyes. Even with his thinning gray hair and generously lined face, no one who paid attention would miss how observant and intelligent the bishop was.

"Father Hall, good to see you enjoying one of London's finger social engagements," he said in a deep, rumbly voice. "I daresay you've caused a bit of a stir."

"I do hope the results will be positive rather than leading me into difficulty, Bishop."

Bishop Bassingham scanned the crowd, now lining themselves up for the first round of dances.

"Positive to my perspective, since they've livened up an otherwise unremarkable winter evening. From what I've heard, seeing such a handsome young clergyman in attendance has raised the quality of the ball considerably, and will surely result in lively discussions for the rest of the week."

Father Hall tried not to laugh and insult his most helpful benefactor and guide to the ways of his new home. He was hardly a callow youth at thirty-four, and he expected his fine blond hair to turn to thinning at any moment. And he considered his features too delicate—too like his sister's, in fact—to ever aspire to handsome.

Better to deflect than quibble, as was often the case.

"Then I'm glad to have made our generous host and hostess happy."

Bishop Bassingham studied Father Hall for a few seconds, eyes narrowed, then nodded to himself. Father Hall wondered what test he had just failed or passed, but only for a second.

"I sought you out to warn you, Father, of a rather odd Frenchwoman who isn't seeking marriage or a dance, and certainly not seeking the acquaintance and comfort of benefactors as you and I are. I'm not exactly certain what she *is* seeking aside from meddling and disruption and inconvenience in the year ahead." He leaned close enough that Father Hall realized the mulled cider had been deemed acceptable from the aroma on his breath.

"I rather expect this young woman will end in scandal for herself and for anyone who associates himself with her. And I hope that will serve as an adequate warning to you, Father. I know of your enjoyment of speaking to many different types of people."

Father Hall smiled, but he knew it was a strained and unnatural affair.

Bishop Bassingham supported his efforts to help down-on-their-luck working men, as did other churches throughout the city. But he'd been confused at Father Hall's interest in seeking to help *anyone* who needed it, in whatever way they needed. He suspected his own superiors in Rome would have been confused and concerned about that if they paid much attention to him or his tiny congregation.

Especially when it came to his modest church's unusually rich collection of research materials.

Histories, records, even fiction, and more than the usual number of maps and expeditionary notes from various parts of the world, all held in the residency across the street from the church itself. Father Hall knew how lucky he'd been to take up leadership at a relatively disadvantaged post with unusual riches.

Almost as if the Church wanted to grant enough materials for the number of parishes it hoped to have someday.

Father Hall had often felt sad at how such wonderful information was hidden away from nearly everyone except himself and the nuns who lived in the residence.

Indeed, the idea of a potentially curious and scandalous young woman set his own curiosity to tuning itself up as surely as the band had done.

"I'll be sure to keep my wits about me, Bishop. Thank you for the word."

Bishop Bassingham lowered his head and raised one bushy gray eyebrow, as if he could see the quietly rebellious thoughts in Father Hall's head, or perhaps the unhealthy desire for disobedience in his heart. But he only nodded again, then set off into the crowd.

At the first quick and spritely notes from two violins, Father Hall decided to seek the refuge of the terrace after all.

But then purposeful movement toward him caught his eye.

And he knew without a doubt that he'd just been spotted by Bishop Bassingham's mysterious Frenchwoman.

If he hadn't been paying close attention—not only to the bishop's description but to the person ignoring the fluttering dancers and striding toward him—Father Hall might have thought her a rather slender man.

She was nearly his height, and her curly brown hair was shorter than many men's. Rather than elaborate gowns the colors of spring flowers still months away, she wore a plain dark green dress. And once she'd noticed him, he had the feeling no amount of chatter or music or impatient dancers would deter her from her course.

When she stopped in front of him, chin held high and expression determined, he noticed she had lovely green eyes that blazed with intelligence. Looking directly into his rather than pretending demure postures that would never have suited her.

No wonder the bishop had been disapproving.

"Father William Hall?" she said in a pleasantly deep voice, her French accent strong but her English clear.

"The very one. How may I be of service to you?"

She blinked, then smiled, transforming her square jaw and pale skin from rather stern to something approaching beautiful.

"I am Dr. Jean Marchér." She pronounced it Zhon Mar-shay, and Father Hall's curiosity took over even more of his mind and customary good sense. "Yes, I am perfectly aware that's normally a man's name. My parents were far more fond of Jeanne than I, so I changed it to suit me. Since they didn't protest, no one else has standing to do so."

How refreshing her directness was after the evening of stuffy introductions and painfully polite imitations of conversation.

Father Hall hesitated for only a second before holding out his hand.

"I'm pleased to meet you, Dr. Marchér. I hope you've had a pleasant holiday season so far."

She shook her head, but flashed that smile again. Her grip was firm and warm.

"No no, please don't call me doctor. I introduce myself that way to make sure your London society types understand to take me seriously. Otherwise they assume I'm only after a husband, which I assure you is the last thing I would ever seek out. My impression that you would start off without the need for such time-wasting games appears to be true. Jean will suffice."

"Very well, Jean. How may I help you?"

She stared at him consideringly, much like Bishop Bassingham had done. She easily raised her voice over the first of the dances starting up at last.

"I hope we may help each other, Father Hall. I've had word that you're a bit of an unusual clergy member, for one thing. A bit of a renegade, to be entirely honest, much like myself. Hopefully not likely to dismiss me and my research efforts out of hand. Also that you're in possession of a most impressive library."

Now Father Hall smiled himself.

"I have no intention of dismissing you at all, as long as you're willing to join me in inappropriate familiarity and call me William. I suppose I *am* unusual in London, for a number of reasons. And my church has been blessed with an abundance of materials. I've often felt it was a shame that no one has been making use of them. What sort of information do you seek?"

Jean glanced over his shoulder toward the terrace, while at the same time, Father Hall noticed Bishop Bassingham watching them. His black cassock stood out through the kaleidoscope of brilliant gowns and dark jackets currently filling the middle of the ballroom in a flurry of motion.

The bishop was too far away to see his face, but Father

Hall had no doubt his expression would be far from approving.

It was just as well he had no authority whatsoever over either Father Hall or his church.

"I suppose no one will overhear us through that infernal noise," Jean said. "I've been fortunate to travel a great deal, William, in search of most unusual customs, beliefs, and rituals. I've found more than I expected, and not nearly as many as I hoped for. Your faith and leaders of your church have long had a great interest about such things, yes?"

"I'm afraid I'm not sure what you mean. There are extensive histories, and our residence has a collection of expeditionary notes that would be the envy of many museums and universities. Are you compiling a history as part of your teaching?"

Jean's eyes lit up, and she leaned forward, clearly warming to her subject and her passion.

"Teaching is not my pursuit, though I've been happy to share my knowledge where appropriate. *Exchanging* knowledge with another is nearly always appropriate. I would be most interested in those expeditionary notes, and perhaps records of rituals within your church. I'm a student of magic, you see, and a beginning practitioner myself."

Father Hall's eyebrows went up without his permission, and he hoped his smile kept him from looking as incredulous as he felt.

And perhaps covered up his growing sense of intrigue.

"Now that *is* interesting, Jean. I myself grew up surrounded by deep beliefs in the fairies and good people in the west of England, and watching my family and everyone else in our village take great care not to upset them. Leaving out offerings and all manner of rituals encouraging their presence. I regret that I never saw evidence of them. Is that the sort of thing you mean?"

Jean shrugged with one shoulder and shook her head, the corners of her mouth turning down.

"I know such things from my own childhood, of course. They're rather pedestrian, don't you think? Compared to the wonders of the world away from our two so-called civilized nations? Surely you studied far more thought-provoking phenomena as part of your training for the priesthood."

Father Hall tried to suppress a shudder without much success.

"I did indeed. The history of our Church contains more wonders, and more horrors, than most people who haven't been initiated into its secrets could possibly know. I doubt I know many of them myself. Please forgive me, we've been talking all this time and I haven't offered you any refreshment. I've been confining myself to water thus far this evening, but I suspect I could do with something more substantial for this conversation."

Jean threw back her head and laughed then, with unfortunate timing at the end of the energetic song. Her hearty exaltation rang throughout the ballroom, generating an echoing wave of polite titters in response.

And the unmistakable opinion of Bishop Bassingham energetically crossing his arms.

"This conversation will only be the beginning should we decide to work together," Jean said. "And there's no reason either of us should suffer their insipid beverages, fit only for a young child with a running nose."

She reached into a fold of her skirt and pulled out a silvery flask no larger than her palm, then nodded toward the half-full glass of water Father Hall had quite forgotten about. He swallowed the rest and held it out. Jean quickly poured a generous three fingers of dark amber liquid for him.

"To a possible new endeavor," she said, holding the flask up between them. Out of view from the rest of the ballroom, but he was quite sure she didn't waste a second worrying about that. "And the beginning of most interesting times for both of us."

Father Hall tilted the glass toward her before he held it up, inhaling deeply of the earthy aroma before he drank it all. The whisky went down surprisingly smooth, with a burning ginger aftertaste.

He doubted he'd ever tasted spirit that fine as he welcomed the lightening of his arms and legs.

And of his concerns about Bishop Bassingham and his overbearing ways.

"Tell me more of this magic you've studied, Jean. And what practices you've taken up."

She raised one eyebrow and held her head to the side.

"You're not worried about spoiling your reputation by speaking to one such as me?"

This time Father Hall laughed, but thankfully the music had started up again. He reflexively looked over her shoulder for the bishop, but he'd moved on.

Perhaps to find another hopeless young soul to save, one that might respond to his efforts.

And thrive under his heavy-handed guidance and control.

"The fact that someone sent you my way, Jean—scandalous as you believe yourself to be—should tell us both all we need to know about *my* reputation within this layer of London society. Aren't you worried about speaking to a man you've just met without a proper chaperone?"

"More than one person sent me your way, so I expect you're correct about your reputation in London. I must tell you all of them spoke of you with admiration, and none of them are in this room. As for my being proper, or meeting anyone's expectations outside of my own, those days ended long before they possibly could have begun. Tell me, does your collection hold anything believed to be cursed? Or even blessed?"

The curiosity drifting along in the whisky warmth in Father Hall's belly quickened into excitement.

He wasn't anyone's prophet or saint, and never aspired to be. But he possessed a steady and reliable sense of which path his life should take in the moment that had never yet steered him wrong. Perhaps inherited from his family and their comfort with truths their ordinary senses couldn't confirm, which in the end wasn't all that different from what the Church taught.

He not only believed Jean could determine the authenticity of the objects in question, but that she'd only revealed the barest beginning of her talents and skills.

"A few things that are rumored to be both blessed and cursed, yes," he said. "I haven't made much of a study of them myself, not as of yet. I'm afraid the collection is barely cataloged or organized in any real sense of the word. The former priest passed on rather suddenly, so I've spent most of my tenure so far trying to work out...well, everything. To tell you the truth, having someone go through it all with a scholar's eye and intellect would be a tremendous help to me."

He stared out at the currents and eddies of young, colorful, wealthy young people before looking into Jean's eyes.

"A help I would prefer to be able to reward you for. But the main reason I'm attending this ball is to build up relationships with the community, at least those who aren't already put off by my apparently colorful reputation. And hopefully inspire those few to support the church and my charity work with the resource they have most of, in exchange for what I inevitably have more of."

"And what would those precious resources be?"

He thought from the twinkle in her eye that she already knew.

"Most individuals in this room have far more money than I ever hope to amass, for myself or for my parish. Despite our wealth of knowledge, the larger Church will never likely see fit to increase our other resources. I in turn have vast amounts more of time, along with discipline, and devotion. To the earthly building itself, and to the spiritual health of the congregation. Most importantly as far as my potential benefactors are concerned, of course, to their ever-lasting souls."

Jean raised her chin and one eyebrow, still ignoring the music and carefully rehearsed rituals going on behind her. Father Hall suspected that, like himself, anything so predictable and uninspiring would ever catch her attention.

"In that case," she said, "I can help solve your difficulty in one area if you'll permit me. My parents have endowed me with a most generous allowance, likely in hopes of my getting all of this stubbornness and lust for travel and education out of my system. I fear redirecting my other lusts and passions into more acceptable channels will continue to prove beyond my abilities."

Jean paused long enough to flash what Father Hall's mother would have called a purely wicked grin before she went on.

"So you needn't worry for my everlasting soul, Father Hall. As I rush ever closer to my thirties and my societal spinsterhood, my parents would much prefer to know I'm happy without having to know how or why. Therefore, money is not one of the earthly needs I struggle with. Much like many of the figures in your Bible, I care far more for learning and living my life than I do for the worldly comforts riches can provide."

Father Hall hesitated long enough to give the appearance of considering her offer, though he wasn't sure why. Dr. Jean Marchér had given him no indication of being the sort of person who cared for appearances, no matter the occasion.

The truth was having a thorough investigation and catalog of the residence's rooms full of papers and maps and objects would be a gift beyond measure, and one he wasn't likely ever to accomplish on his own. A gift to his tiny church and parish, to everyone who dwelled or worshiped there in the future, and of course to the Church, even if Rome would be better off not knowing much about the architect of that gift.

And the gift to himself? Of knowledge, both worldly and possibly of realms not visible to his earthly senses? And of a friend who shared his troublesome curiosity, and of not caring so much for the opinions of others as he likely should?

That would be the true blessing, and one he could never hope to repay.

Except with his own friendship in return.

"I believe we can come to an agreement that will greatly benefit us both," he said. "And from what you've gathered, raising both our reputations as eccentrics is both more obtainable and more desirable than any further efforts at living conventional lives."

Jean's irresistible laugh rang out again, sadly buried under the insistent music and conversation filling the ballroom.

"I agree on every point," she said. "We appear to be very well met indeed. So shall I join you at your church tomorrow? We'll speak after your mass, of course, though I may sit in for curiosity's sake. Then I expect we'll discover at least some of those items both cursed and blessed will prove more than rumors under my magical tests."

Father Hall knew his own grin at that prospect would have been deemed quite wicked indeed by his mother, and likely downright threatening by Bishop Bassingham.

And he found to his delight that he simply did not care.

"Then I'll see you tomorrow, Jean, for that meeting of our renegade minds. And we'll get our adventures together well and truly underway."

CHRIS TOOK IN A DEEP, slow breath, focusing on the entirely different input of his senses as he drifted out of Victorian London and back into modern-day Lightning Gap, Virginia.

He no longer stood in the middle of a crowded ballroom full of women in gowns so elaborate that they surpassed the most creative cosplay or Hollywood costume dramas, with the men in tailcoats wearing watch chains that had to cause back pain.

He no longer felt the curious and daring freedom of a long black cassock, and thankfully he'd shed the constricting collar. He and everyone else safe and snug in the basement of Odds and Endings wore a brilliant variety of soft, comfortable clothing that would have been far more scandalous on that long-ago evening than Father Hall and Jean Marchér sharing whisky.

The peaty aroma of that illicit tipple faded, shifting to the warm, crackling fire. He caught the Seagons' clove-studded oranges and a hint of Mr. Seagon's wonderful ginger cookies, along with an entirely welcome whiff of BeeGirl's eau de hound dog.

BeeGirl was actually awake and staring straight at him, her pleading brown eyes matched only by her thumping red tail.

With a back-to-reality start, Chris realized BeeGirl's human Ivy and her best friend Venus were looking at him too, along with the Seagons, and Kay and Adam from the café across the street.

When the distant violins, viola, and cello creating the tempo for a mid-holiday Victorian ball finally drifted away from his senses, he understood why all those eyes were turned his way.

Everyone in the cozy leather chairs in the magical room full of books were cheering and applauding him. For telling a story, rather than his usual role of help EllaJane spin the yarn.

And EllaJane herself sat beside him with the biggest smile of all, wiping a quick tear away from her lovely brown eyes.

"That was wonderful, Chris," Mrs. Seagon said. "I adore tales of side characters, especially from worlds I've traveled before. Authors who let those characters come to life rather than reducing them to moving chess pieces are always better for it, as are their stories. From the looks of you right now, I'd say you had no idea you were such a storyteller yourself."

Chris laughed, shaking his head and blinking. Even working with EllaJane—living out the stories as they told them together—hadn't given him a clue he had anywhere near the same ability.

"I have to admit I didn't have a clue," he said. "EllaJane helped me every step of the way, or I never would have known."

He turned to her again, and the pride and joy in her eyes had him struggling to keep himself from reaching for her hand.

"I might have helped you, Chris, but that story was your own. It was a real pleasure discovering it with you."

Before Chris could manage to recover his suddenly lost words, taken from him by the affection in her eyes, Mr. Seagon rescued him.

"As is so often the case, we're all better off when two such well-matched people find themselves together. I know our mystery author will be thrilled with this addition to such a rich and fascinating world. *We* certainly are."

"And we're more excited than ever to hear the next tale," Mrs. Seagon said, clasping her hands together across her purple-clad middle. "Always assuming you can work your way across the street through the snow."

Kay sat forward in her sky-blue footie pajamas with a big grin.

"Y'all better work your way across first thing in the morning for the breakfast I'm going to whip up for all of us. I only make eggnog French toast during this week, and you don't want to miss it."

At that, everyone started gathering themselves up, getting ready to head up out of the basement. The Seagons to their rooms adjacent to the wonderful sprawl of the bookstore, and Ivy, BeeGirl, Venus, Kay, and Adam for their chilly trek through the blizzard.

Chris thanked his lucky stars that all he needed to do was stagger a few yards to his apartment and crash for the night. Telling the tale had taken more effort than he expected.

And given him more than he'd ever imagined.

"Did you have a single word of that planned, Chris?" EllaJane said, and her expression was as admiring at her words.

"Not a single one. Much as it terrified me, you were right. The story told itself to me. All I had to do was get out of the way. I'm still a lot more suited to being a character, but I wouldn't mind a bit more practice from this side of the world."

She smiled and leaned toward him, and Chris very much wished they were alone.

"Then we'll make that happen. Our adventure is only beginning, too."

KARI KILGORE

AUTHOR OF WHEN THE FOG CLEARS AND A BLIZZARD IN PINK

The Real Gift
Of the Santa Train

For everyone who finds the best gifts
by helping others

THE REAL GIFT OF THE
SANTA TRAIN

ELLAJANE COLE SETTLED herself in for the third night of
the Odds and Endings Mid-Holiday Madness with a pleasant
bit of soreness in her muscles that she hadn't experienced
since she was a kid. The direct result of a bright, refreshingly
cold day full of sledding, snow-based construction, snowball
fights, and generous helpings of hot chocolate.

The entire town of Lightning Gap, Virginia, had gotten
in on the fun of a post-Christmas, pre-New Year's snow day.

With two feet on the ground and a comfortable certainty
that the road down off the mountain would be blocked for at
least one more day, everyone agreed that plowing wouldn't
make much sense with so much fun to be had. So by the
time everyone finally admitted the winter-early sunset was
calling a halt to the festivities, Lightning Gap's main street
was a wonderland of snow citizens dressed in all sorts of
bizarre finery.

Everything from old bridesmaid dresses to t-shirts and
shorts, with almost every exposed bit of "skin" dyed with a
rainbow of colors. Turned out beet juice, blueberry juice, tea,

and all kinds of other concoctions and mixes EllaJane had never considered created quite the variety of shades.

Little frozen groups gathered around similarly brightened versions of campfires, dogs and cats, and freeform, multi-hued sculptures so lovely it was a shame they'd be gone in a day or two. A huge cup of perfectly dark-brown snow-coffee beside a plate of multi-colored cookies invited folks into Kay's Café across the street. And of course, the contented group of winter-only patrons outside of the Odds and Endings Bookstore held icy versions of books, with stacks more beside them for their overnight reading pleasure.

It was the fortifications and daring sledding runs down by the high school—close under the sheltering ridge with the towering Lightning Rock standing guard—that had delighted and exhausted EllaJane. She'd spent the same kind of endless hours building and climbing and sliding and throwing as she had as a kid.

With a noticeably different result on her early forties body, but nothing a long, hot, lavender-scented bath in her apartment in the Odds and Endings basement couldn't set right.

That along with sitting on a soft leather sofa in front of the basement's gorgeous fireplace, her extra-fluffy red comforter covered with impressions of holly and mistletoe tucked around her legs, and a cup of Carabelle Seagon's special warming tea helped along with a generous splash of bourbon.

Not that being in a vast basement entirely dedicated to books wouldn't have soothed EllaJane's mind, body, and soul without a drop to drink. The fire's cheery yellow light flick-ered against the purple and green fireplace tiles and rows of dark wooden bookshelves, highlighting the wondrous variety of colors, bindings, and subjects of the millions of words all around her.

A treasure of stories that EllaJane and her increasingly close friend and character Chris were engaged in adding to over the year of their residency.

The book-loving group gathered around her were similarly blanket-draped and beverage-equipped, all of them happily engaged in describing their own snow days before the storytelling began. Between the fire, all the beverages, and all that glorious paper, the whole basement always smelled like heaven.

Adding in the gorgeous tree, bunches of citrus studded with cloves, and loops of fresh pine garland turned the volume up to winter holiday paradise.

Carabelle and her husband Arthur, the owners of Odds and Endings, had brought out yet another of their matching pairs of sweatshirts and pants, hers in the same purple as the house, his in a warm chocolate brown. Tonight they were decorated with glittering images of poinsettias with dark green leaves, intensely red flowers, and brilliant yellow centers.

Ivy Gweddon and her sweet redbone hound BeeGirl were both dressed in matching bright-green sweaters covered with embroidered gifts wrapped in a dizzying array of colors and metallic accents. Quite the departure from Ivy's normal wardrobe of sturdy tans.

Ivy's best friend Venus Mullins—curled up on the other side of BeeGirl with a satisfied smile—had presented the sweaters with obvious glee and absolutely no remorse.

Which made sense, because she'd traded in her usual world-traveler-fabulous attire for the same sweater in electric blue.

EllaJane had made detailed mental notes of Ivy's impressive stream of foul language as she outfitted BeeGirl, then herself, in the festive clothing. Along with Ivy's affectionate smiles and a big hug and kiss for Venus.

BeeGirl might be snoring now, but she'd been equally appreciative and demonstrative in the moment.

The owner of Kay's Café and her husband Adam had arrived in matching pairs of hot-pink footie pajamas, after a busy day serving up gallons of delicious hot chocolate, cold-chasing soup, and appetite-quenching chili. And they'd managed to hold aside a plateful of decadent and spicy cheese and sausage balls to go along with Mr. Seagon's wonderful crispy ginger cookies.

And all of the friendly chatter and great food and weary muscles in the world couldn't quite distract EllaJane from Chris sitting beside her. He'd livened up his usual black sweatpants and t-shirt wardrobe with a sparkling golden scarf that brought out the highlights in his brilliant green eyes.

He sat a bit closer than he had the night before, when he'd taken his own wonderful turn as bard for the evening, sharing a perfectly timed tale of two kindred souls finding each other.

EllaJane found she wished he'd scoot on over and eliminate the distance altogether.

A curious and entirely pleasant sensation that couldn't help but play into the story taking shape in her mind even when she tried to steer her subconscious in another direction.

Chris seemed to look her way more often than over the past few weeks they'd been writing and playing and creating together. Leaning toward her as he recounted his own flying-snowball-filled day. Elbow brushing against hers, cross-legged knee touching hers, then leaving her disappointed when he moved away.

Besides her own tingling internal fireworks and Chris's ever-more confident hints, EllaJane couldn't help noticing the way everyone else watched the two of them. Speculative and knowing smiles combined with nostalgic sighs to make it clear she hadn't imagined a thing unfolding between them.

Not to mention the fascinating bits of history she'd discovered before everyone arrived, as the reliable magic of Odds and Endings served up exactly what she was looking for.

A reassuring percentage of author/character partnerships begun in this very basement had turned into more permanent arrangements over the years.

A number EllaJane was more than willing to consider adding to before all was said and done.

At the unusual and traditional moment of eleven minutes past the hour, Carabelle Seagon got to her feet, and everyone except BeeGirl quieted down. She continued her burst of eerie dog-dream barking.

"I trust everyone had a fantastic play-in-the-snow day," she said, beaming. "We certainly did. This was the most lovely snowfall we've had in Lightning Gap for at least ten years. I expect everyone in town has enough photos and memories to keep it alive until our next winter wonderland comes calling. So without further introduction, I'll turn the floor over to EllaJane and Chris, and their next tale from the worlds of our mysterious Odds and Endings author."

EllaJane smiled at the burst of applause, and laughed along when BeeGirl raised her head, looked around with a clear air of disapproval, and flopped back down again.

"I'm not sure how many of you are still in the dark about our author," she said, "but we appreciate you playing along. If you are still wondering, Chris and I worked in advance with our fellow Odds and Endings creator to pick out New Year's Eve gifts that will lead right back into these wonderful worlds. We both appreciate you not sneaking a peek under the tree in advance, at least not where we can see you."

She turned to Chris, as she had so many times, and *this* time his smile took her breath away. Something about the promise in his eyes.

A promise her own heart, body, and mind wanted to help him keep.

"Tonight we're heading down the mountain and over to Estonoa," he said. "For a much-loved tradition in Appalachia. And I get the feeling we'll be enjoying an even more loved tradition in holiday storytelling, from short stories to novels to lots of TV shows and movies. I don't mind admitting I'm looking forward to this one myself."

EllaJane paused long enough to catch her breath, or at least to try.

In that moment, looking into his eyes, no one else existed, in the room and the town and anywhere else in the world.

"Then let's see what happens," she finally said.

And because the time for waiting had come to an end, EllaJane launched into the tale, with Chris close by her side.

THE DAY of the Santa Train's arrival in Estonoa, Virginia, dawned cloudy and overcast, but Susan McFarland refused to let the November gloom sink into her own mood. Even if the forecast proved out and the gray-bellied clouds made good on the snow she smelled in the air, that would only bring a little bit more joy to the occasion.

The truth was she absolutely refused to let her first turn as chair of the official welcoming committee go off as anything other than a spectacular success.

And she was going to do everything she possibly could to hold on to that sense of optimism no matter how the day turned out.

The first thing that meant was arriving downtown unreasonably early to make sure the committee's hard work in creating a reasonable facsimile of a winter wonderland hadn't suffered during the strong winds overnight.

Which was the only thing that could *possibly* explain her standing in an empty parking lot beside the railroad tracks at seven on a Saturday morning, clutching a stainless-steel Clinch River Books tankard in one hand and the loose knot of an extra-long pink scarf in the other. Doing her level best to warm up, wake up, and keep the overly brisk and ambitious wind from *picking* her up and carrying her away.

Maybe to a place where someone else might take over and deal with this mess.

The silver of the tracks up on their own steep, rock-covered little hill stood out against the winter-gray circle of the mountains around Estonoa, seeming to draw a line connecting the tan brick building of a law office and town museum on one side to the red brick bank and post office on the other.

Funny how the things people needed consolidated themselves closer together in a small town, rather than sprawling all over the place like in a big city.

When Susan had finally headed home late the night before, a wonderful little Santa's village had been tucked up sweet and cozy against the museum building, waiting to entertain waiting children and adults alike. She and the other volunteers had hung a groovy impressionistic mural supplied by the high school art department, with holiday trees painted in green and blue and purple, silver and gold and white, all reaching almost as high as the three stories of the building and twice that far across.

At the base of the mural's adorable depiction of snow-covered roads and houses, they'd added in enough miniature buildings painted to match to create the appearance of walking *into* the scene.

Fluffy cotton batting on the roofs and little brick walls,

with space for toys and games inside. They'd even set up a precious tiny art studio so the kids (and adults who were willing to play along) could paint their very own stockings and plastic ornaments to take home.

As it turned out, a gust of the very same wind that was working overtime to rip Susan's cheery pink scarf away and turn her curly brown hair into a riot of static had already had its wicked way with the mural.

Which now draped itself ever so gracefully across their tiny village, and half the parking lot for good measure.

Susan closed her eyes yet again, as if removing the whole thing from view could somehow return her to the giddy excitement of the night before, working by portable spot-lights to get the finishing touches into place.

Thank goodness they'd taken the big, expensive lights back inside the museum before heading out for the night.

She dared opening one eye, just a peek.

Nope.

Nothing but the unlovely, off-white side of a gigantic canvas as far as her eyes could see, rumpled into hundreds of hills and valleys nowhere near as interesting as the now-invis-ible village.

Susan took a long drink of her coffee, thankful to her best friend Will for hooking her up with a heavy dose of hot chocolate to mix in. Every extra boost of energy she could get and more was welcome.

Because nothing was going to stop the Santa Train from rolling into Estonoa at precisely 10:23, following the same historic route it had for nearly a hundred years. Rumbling its way through the mountains, through long night-dark tunnels and across soaring high trestles. Delivering holiday cheer throughout a region that had far too often been in desper-ately short supply of any kind of joy.

Susan had seen the special exhibit in the museum

weeks ago with the whole planning committee, all of them struck into silence by how much the train had meant years ago.

Black-and-white photos of faces too worn and thin on children and adults alike. Holding out their hands for a scattering of hard candy and the only wrapped presents they'd get. Brilliant smiles at the simplest kindness and trace of consideration.

Now the train served a population more nostalgic than desperate, though she didn't doubt more than one family welcomed the chance to add to their meager supplies. Volunteers worked hard along the whole route, giving out backpacks full of stuffed animals, books, and school supplies that surely went a long way.

Later today, whether she and Estonoa were ready or not, cheering crowds would greet Santa waving from the back of the caboose, and smile and laugh and chat with everyone who literally kept the train rolling.

Celebration rather than desperation.

Susan shivered as an especially energetic gust of damp wind slithered past her scarf and darted up the legs of her jeans and into the sleeves of her Estonoa High sweatshirt.

But more than that wind brought on the shiver, and did every single year. Waiting in nearly this exact spot, she'd always gotten caught up in her own wave of joy mixed with sorrow, even before seeing all those eyes gazing out of the past in the museum.

Something about that lonesome sound of the train whistle echoing long before it arrived, and the way the rails sang under the wheels got to her every time.

She did her best to chase the advance blues away with another long swallow of chocolate-laced coffee, then risked her scarf finally managing to untie itself by reaching into her hip pocket for her phone. Before she got her chilled fingers to the screen, movement on the train tracks caught her attention.

Not people walking down the tracks, arriving extra-early like she half expected. Avoiding the rush before the serious parking crunch all across town got started.

Instead a white pickup truck with the dark green logo of the railroad on the side rolled along the tracks, a pair of bright orange warning lights rotating on top. Despite her disappointment and dread of figuring out what to do next, Susan grinned.

She'd seen the hi-rail trucks most of her life, but they still looked odd up there. Like a toy car might speeding along an interstate highway. Tiny versions of dark metal train wheels extended past the regular wheels, attached to much heavier than usual bumpers front and back.

She waved the hand holding her phone without thinking, and the scarf took that moment to finally slip its knot and set half of its length free to stream out behind her.

Susan laughed and grabbed at the remaining end with her coffee-holding hand, thankful she'd flipped the lid closed. By the time she managed to get her phone back in her pocket and reel her merry pink escape artist back in, she heard footsteps and an answering laugh getting closer.

"Almost got away from you there, but that was an impressive catch."

The extremely old-school type in a pinstriped locomotive engineer's cap over silver hair and a bright smile who always drove those trucks in her mind wasn't there at all.

In fact the African-American man walking toward her wasn't wearing any kind of hat, and his jeans and green railroad employee jacket fit a heck of a lot better than the engineer's coveralls in Susan's imagination. The silver hair was nowhere to be found, either, having been replaced by a neat cap of close-trimmed black hair with a matching goatee.

And that smile, the way it lit up his dark brown eyes?

Way better than the kind of Santa-jolly, grandfatherly man she'd imagined.

Susan took a quick bow as she wrangled the scarf back around her head.

"Why thank you. I might have fumbled it if I'd known I had an audience. Are you inspecting the tracks ahead of the Santa Train?"

"Sure am. I volunteer to do this every year to help make sure everything goes well. Started out before the sun came up with my headlights on. This is the one day a year we actually have to worry about having an audience in all these towns. I suspect most folks don't pay attention to the trains passing at all, but everyone seems to love this one as much as I do."

Susan shrugged, and she felt shy with no idea what had come over her. She generally was *anything* but the shy type.

"I always notice them, ever since I was a kid, but this one is my favorite. My grandfather worked for the railroad over in Wolf Branch, so I got to see trains a lot growing up. I kinda hated it when they stopped pulling cabooses and there was no one I could wave to."

He leaned his head back and laughed, and it was the best sound Susan had heard for a good long while. Deep and hearty, and coming from his whole body.

"So *that's* why you waved. I wasn't sure whether you were trying to get my attention so I could help chase down your scarf or help figure out what went wrong with your mural there."

The jolt back to earth was hard enough that Susan winced before she could stop herself.

"Yeah, it's a mess, huh? I have no idea how in the world I'm going to get it straightened up before the train comes through." She stared out at the wrinkles and folds of canvas, with the thickest piles over the invisible winter village. Then she turned back to the handsome stranger. "Wait, how did you know it was a mural? Surely this isn't a common enough occurrence that you've seen it before."

He shook his head and turned toward the mess, hands on his hips.

"Can't say that I've seen this before, no. But I did see the town's pictures on social media last night. I was planning to circle back here in time to watch the train go through. I try to pick a different town each year just to see the crowds. It was an easy choice this year, with everything looking so great."

Susan smiled, knowing the fake expression was hardly her best look. Pretending to be happy was something that had never come naturally to her.

She'd decided years ago that she was glad about that.

"Well, thank you for saying so. I'm afraid the kids and everyone else will be disappointed. Probably shouldn't have posted those photos, huh? I'm Susan McFarland, by the way."

He turned back to her at once and held out his hand. Susan's fit into it perfectly, and she suspected the tingle working its way through her body wasn't only because his hand was so wonderfully warm.

"Paul Carslon, glad to meet you, Susan. Listen, I'd bet I can get some of our local folks to help you out. A bunch of us are on-call for the big day anyway. Just in case your committee can't get together in time. I've got family from Estonoa, so I've always loved it here. Happy to help if I can."

Susan blinked, and her own slow smile felt wonderful and entirely natural this time. Paul didn't look like he felt sorry for her or like he thought the whole situation was ridiculous, even though Susan was quite sure she'd cackle about it with her friends over at the bookstore in town later on.

He simply looked concerned. Like he actually cared about this little town and the people who planned to show up today to celebrate.

And damn, didn't that concern look *fantastic* on him.

"Okay, let me first clear my familial and cultural obligation," she said, "and insist that while I appreciate the offer, you sure don't have to go to all that trouble. Then I'll immediately add that if you have some strong and cheerful railroad folks to call in, that would be a tremendous help. I can pay them in killer hot chocolate from the bookstore in town, and some of the best divinity, homemade marshmallows, and potato candy you've ever tasted."

Paul grinned and pulled a phone out of his pocket.

"You're on, especially for all that sugary goodness. My granny made those when I was a kid, and store-bought never did taste anywhere near as good. Let me see who all I can round up."

He took a couple of steps to the side and started tapping away, leaving Susan shaking her head. Sure, she could get at least a few people here on short notice, but most of them would be either hard to reach or wouldn't be able to get away.

If they got a big enough crew together, they just might be able to pull this thing off.

And the idea of spending a bit more time getting to know Paul certainly would brighten up her day.

She got her phone back out and started rounding up her own recruits.

PAUL CARLSON WALKED in a small circle across the parking lot in Estonoa, making sure he looked at the tan brick building, the tragically crumpled mural at the bottom, and out at his Chevy on the tracks in turn.

Mainly to keep himself from staring at the gorgeous woman talking on her phone several feet away. He hadn't expected to see anyone out this early today, since he'd made this long inspection drive in peaceful solitude for years now.

But if there was ever a fantastic way for a habit to change, even one he loved and looked forward to, this had to be it.

He could see where the pulleys had slipped at the top of the three-story building, and thankfully the ropes seemed to all still be there. Getting it all put back together again should be fairly simple once they had enough people to keep everything from tangling up. That and someone to let them into the building and onto the roof.

The photos he'd seen the night before would have been reason enough to want to help. The mural's colorful trees soaring above the absurdly cute little village created a scene he wished he could step into himself.

The idea of kids and their families alike not being able to enjoy that simply would not do.

And if he happened to get a chance to spend more time with Susan, who had somehow captured every bit of his attention in a way no one had for longer than he cared to think about?

He'd be a fool to pass that up, even without the promise of hot chocolate, divinity, and marshmallows thrown in.

There was the reply he'd been waiting for. Billy McShane would be happy to not only come downtown to help, but he was also glad to finish up the inspection drive. Then loop the truck back around since he lived in Estonoa and wanted to see the train himself.

Leaving Paul free to do his best to recreate that heart-melting smile of Susan's as often as he possibly could.

He turned and almost crashed right into her, and that did the trick.

"Oh, I'm sorry!" she said, drawing back, but not before Paul caught the enticing aroma of her hair, still trying to escape from the cutest pink scarf on the planet. "I didn't mean to sneak up on you like that. I've got six people on the way, and my friend Will promised to bring coffee and hot chocolate. We may have to wait on the sugary treats, but help will be here in about five minutes."

"Hey, that's great! I've got four guys headed in, should be here not long after that. A couple of them are bringing tools in case the village needs a bit of a remodel."

Susan closed her eyes and held one hand over her heart, which gave Paul time to swoon a bit over how beautiful she looked, even in the overcast morning light.

"I hadn't even *thought* of that. I'm sure all those yards of canvas did some damage." She glanced toward his truck. "Listen, this is going to sound like a strange question, but I figure I've got you here for at least a minute or two before you need to go finish up your inspection. How do you keep from going off the rails in one of those trucks?"

Paul laughed. "It's not strange at all if you've never driven one. Once I get it lined up on the tracks and drop the metal wheels, I lock the steering out altogether. Then it steers exactly like a train, which I don't mind one bit going over those big trestles. The last thing I'd want would be to derail myself a few hundred feet up."

He paused, not sure if he'd overstepped on arranging to have someone else do the inspection or not. It had certainly seemed like a great idea at the time.

But wow, what if Susan got the idea he was some kind of demented railroad stalker? Or just flat out didn't want to stand around talking to him before everyone else showed up?

"You look like you're trying to figure out an annoying

problem," she said, a small frown curving her lovely red lips down. "It's okay if you need to go ahead. I can handle everything here."

"No, it's fine. I mean, of course you can handle it, you got it all planned and set up, right? I was just... I've got another guy who can take over the inspection. In fact he wants to. If that's okay with you, if I stay here and help?"

Susan shook her head, and for a second, Paul was ready to sprint back to the truck and get out of there. Limited by the rather slow speeds he could manage on the tracks, but anyway.

Then her brilliant grin broke through.

"I'm sorry, you bet it's okay with *me* if you stay. That would be great. I was just thinking I'd like to... We could really use the help."

She abruptly looked away, apparently overcome with the need to examine the sadly defeated mural. But Paul's middle warmed up considerably at the sight of her much softer smile and a sweet flush coloring her cheeks.

"Good," he said. "I doubt we can do much until the others get here, not as heavy as that canvas looks. What I want to know more about is the bookstore, specifically that potato candy you mentioned."

Just as he'd hoped, Susan turned back to him, eyes bright and excited.

"That's from my own granny's recipe, and you'll just have to taste it to believe it. I don't know if anyone could ever call potato and sugar dough rolled around homemade peanut butter filling healthy, but it surely is good for the soul this time of year. The divinity we've got in all kinds of flavors, including some a couple of friends brought back from living in Seattle for years."

Paul's stomach, admittedly ready for something more substantial after his quick pre-dawn breakfast, rumbled a good bit more than necessary. Loud enough to hear over the increasingly snow-smelling breeze still working hard to sneak itself under the edges of the defeated mural.

"If you tell me any of those flavors involve coffee, cherries, or apples, my heart might not be able to take it."

Susan giggled and stepped forward to touch Paul's arm, and the weak feeling in his knees definitely was *not* from hunger.

"Then I won't tell you any of that. But I won't go so far as saying none of it is true."

She looked up at him, and the eye contact chased every trace of hunger out of his grumbly belly and replaced it with a thousand cartwheeling butterflies. For her part, Susan's lips parted and she drew in a slow breath.

The sound of a car pulling into the parking lot broke what Paul felt sure was turning into an extremely pleasant spell.

Susan squeezed his arm and glanced over her shoulder.

"There's Will and Chris with the emergency provisions," she said, her voice deeper than it had been before. "I expect the whole crowd will be right behind them. Maybe we'll get a chance to talk more later?"

As if to prove her right, a blue pickup truck rolled in, with Paul's buddy Billy behind the wheel. Paul let out a breath that didn't quite calm his inner cartwheels and smiled.

"I sure do hope so. Let's see what we can't get done to save your mural before the real crowd starts showing up."

After holding his gaze for a few more intense seconds, Susan half-smiled and headed toward the only vehicle in the lot besides Billy's truck. Two guys got out of a gray minivan with Clinch River Books printed on the side in burgundy, immediately grinning at Susan.

Paul forced himself to look away as Billy strolled up to him, ready for the day with his own green railroad jacket and a black toboggan pulled down to his eyebrows. Energetic blond curls escaped it all around, and his reddish beard stood out shocking in the pre-snow morning.

"You feeling okay, Paul? Thought they'd have to pull up the rails to get you to give up this inspection gig." Billy flashed his usual grin and clapped Paul on the shoulder.

"Naaah, feeling just fine. I thought it might be time to toss you a bone since you'll never catch my years of service."

Billy had started barely a year later than Paul, and they'd been fast friends ever since. To the point that Paul had stood up for Billy at his wedding about ten years back, and even sat with his family in the waiting room when all three of Billy's kids were born.

So Paul should have known better than to think Billy wouldn't notice what was going on. Especially once Paul couldn't resist a glance toward the minivan at Susan's joyful laughter.

"Uh-*huh*. Just doing an old friend a favor, right?" Billy peeked for a second himself, then turned back with a wide-eyed, I've-got-a-secret expression. "I'd be happy to introduce you to Will, runs the bookstore here in town and does a hell of a good job. Even better since he hooked up with Chris. You know how it is once a guy falls for someone. Especially a damn fine woman. Livens things up."

Paul rolled his eyes, but he couldn't keep from smiling.

"Yeah, yeah, I remember how it was with you. Turned you into an addle-brained fool is what it did. Anyway, the main thing is to get you out to finish the inspection so I can help get things straightened out here."

He waved one hand at the pitiful pile of canvas, but he knew the distraction wouldn't work, even before Billy confirmed he'd only made it worse.

"Oh, you mean the mural that Susan McFarland over there

got arranged? Real shame how the wind took it out and all. She's head of the committee this year, so anyone who helps her pull things together is sure to gain a *lot* of points in her eyes. From the looks of you, you wouldn't mind that one little bit."

Paul snorted and shook his head, but he couldn't deny a word. Not to someone who knew him so damn well.

"No, I wouldn't mind, smartass. So I'm sure you'll spend the whole ride out contemplating exactly what I'll owe you for this little favor. Never mind that you've been wanting to make this run for years now."

Billy fixed him with a fake glare for several seconds, eyebrows drawn low and mouth pooched out, then he gave up and went back to the grin.

"Awww hell, you got me there. Just let me grab my coffee and I'll get headed out." He ducked his head and leaned closer. "And for the record, Susan is a real sweetheart. Probably deserves better than your sorry ass, but I still think it's a fine idea. Past time, too."

Then he turned and sauntered back toward his truck, tipping his toboggan toward Susan and the two men heading Paul's way.

Leaving Paul with a woefully inadequate few seconds to gather his thoughts before The Friend Audition began.

Susan resisted the urge to fan her face, or perhaps clutch at her heart the same way she'd grabbed the rebellious scarf earlier. Neither Will nor Chris would need help seeing what a state she was in, and she truly did need to get everyone started on The Great Mural Rescue Project.

But *lordy*, the way Paul stared into her eyes just then had put her in a pure tizzy.

One she wanted to find out more about as soon as she possibly could.

Not one bit of any of that changed the fact that the Santa Train would arrive at exactly 10:23 whether she, Estonoa, or her currently invisible holiday village were ready or not.

Bless their hearts, Will and Chris were already walking toward her, Will holding another stainless-steel Clinch River Books tankard full of chocolate-and-coffee-scented goodness.

Just a few months into their relationship, Will and Chris had reached the dressing-alike stage. Making them even more absurdly adorable than they already were. Will's red hair and beard were up to ran-my-fingers-through-it standards, but no one would notice with his gorgeous flannel-shirted lumberjack thing going on.

Chris had himself far more presentable, with his brown hair looking like he was on vacation rather than just waking up ten minutes ago. And yes, of course, his flannel and jeans closely resembled Will's. Blue versus brown was about the only difference she spotted.

Susan decided to let the chance to comment on that go in exchange for that sip of ambrosia.

"Oh hon, what a mess," Will said, handing the coffee over and staring at the rumpled mural. "I'm so sorry. Besides getting you and everyone else tanked up on caffeine, what can we do to help?"

Was it possible he was going to miss the flush Susan could feel in her cheeks?

And she was pretty sure he'd hear her heart galloping away if he stood too close.

"The caffeine will make a huge difference," she said. "Got a few more people on the way from the decorating committee, and more from the railroad believe it or not."

Chris raised one eyebrow and tilted his head.

"Railroad? How in the world did you swing that? I can

barely remember seeing the Santa Train when I was a kid, but I thought they'd all be busy with that."

Now the heat in Susan's cheeks and her whole face turned up to positively blazing. She'd never been good at fibbing her way past Will, or distracting him away from something juicy.

And damn the luck if Chris wasn't every bit as observant.

"Well, they need to get an inspection of the rails done, but wasn't that Billy McShane heading out to take care of that now?"

All three of them turned, and Billy was indeed heading toward the rails and the hi-rail truck. Just then he detoured to throw a playful elbow at Paul, who dodged with his hands flung high in the air and a deep, booming laugh that Susan couldn't help smiling at.

"Yeah," Will said, drawling the word out into at least three syllables. "That sure is Billy, who you would no doubt recognize without any kind of difficulty since we went to high school together. I think the question, Susan my dear, is who is that *other* handsome fellow who keeps looking this way?"

Chris picked up the cue as if they'd been playing this game for years rather than months.

"I do believe he's checking Susan out. Or else he's after you, Will. Either way, I've been living away for decades now. Is the correct procedure to yell about it, or does a menacing glare suffice?"

"I think he's checking *you* out, Chris," Will said. "Can't say that I blame him. Since I don't know the gentleman's name, I think we'll have to go with glares. Wouldn't want to look silly. Shall we practice?"

When both Will and Chris demonstrated glowers far more hilarious than scary, Susan couldn't stop a laugh from bubbling its way out.

"Okay, enough of you two acting a fool. His name is

Paul, and he was doing the inspection. But he called Billy in to take over so he could stay and help get the mural and the village put back together."

Will and Chris grinned at each other before they both stepped closer to Susan.

"Oh, this *is* interesting," Chris said. "Changed all his plans to help out, huh?"

"We'd better go check him out," Will chimed in. "Make sure he's worthy of our Susan. Or, honestly, maybe we should make sure he knows what he might be getting himself into."

And the two of them trooped across the parking lot, leaving Susan scrambling to catch up.

She made it just in time to step in front. She didn't think they would actually jump in and say something mortifying, but she wouldn't bet against it.

Certainly not once she got another look at Paul's gorgeous eyes, and that *smile*.

"Paul Carlson, these are my friends Will Powell and Chris Higgens. Will runs the bookstore here in town, and Chris just moved back home from Seattle."

Paul stepped in with a solid handshake for both Will and Chris, and an amazingly quick wink at Susan.

"Good to meet you both. I've already heard about your coffee, and rumors about all kinds of sweets for later. I saw what happened with the mural overnight on my way by and figured Susan might need a little help. She did such a great job getting everything set up."

Will raised one eyebrow and nodded with an approving smile.

"She sure did. You called in reinforcements too?"

"Couple of guys, yeah, and one with enough carpenter skills to handle any damage to the village." He cast an admiring gaze toward Susan, who did her best to keep from swooning in front of her incredibly annoying friends. "The kids are going to love it all."

Thank all the deities of timing and Susan's poor, over-worked guardian angel, three more vehicles pulled in then. And the office manager from the law office and museum turned down the street on foot right after, with the all-important building keys that would give them access to the roof and those traitorous pulleys.

"We'll just barely have time to get it all set back up if we're lucky," she said. "Because that train's gonna roll through whether we're ready or not."

"We'll be ready if we work together," Paul said with a confident nod. "Once we get your mural back where it belongs, the rest should go pretty quickly. We'll get it exactly the way you want it, Susan."

Will and Chris exchanged raised-eyebrow looks, but followed up with the incredibly unusual choice to refrain from saying something truly embarrassing.

"We're ready," Will said. "And we've got enough fuel in the van for everyone, and more back at the bookstore for later."

At the sight of two more trucks, each with more than one person inside, a painful knot in Susan's shoulders relaxed. Even if the village was flattened, it would still look great.

With any kind of luck—like the luck that had sent Paul driving along just when she needed a distraction—the wind would continue to die down and let them get everything arranged.

Susan was even willing to push it a tiny bit further and hope for a lovely dusting of snow.

"Okay," she said with a grin. "Let's rebuild this here winter wonderland."

≈

ONCE EVERYONE GOT GOING, Paul was amazed at how quickly the work went. Especially with a generous dose of the best coffee he'd tasted in ages in the tanks to keep him going full steam ahead.

Less than an hour got the mural pulled back up into its place of honor, and he realized the photos he'd seen online nowhere near did it justice. They hadn't shown the sparkle painted into the snow and the decorations, or the many shades in each tree and even in the dark blue sky.

The effect against the gray overhead as it finally started to spit snow was magical.

By the time the parking lot and the rest of Estonoa started to fill up, the winter village was restored and ready to go. Only a few miniature roofs needed repair, and a couple of the brick walls picked up and re-attached to their bases.

Thank goodness the incredibly cute supplies of ornaments and stockings and paint for the art studio had been stored inside the law office.

With a quick pass through to fluff up the cotton snow—slowly picking up a layer of the real thing—and the kids and adults charged right in with laughter and smiles all around.

The first distant, lonely sound of the Santa Train's whistle brought all the village activity to a halt, and the resulting shouts of joy brought a nostalgic tear to Paul's eye. As they always did on this special day, his childhood memories seemed to blend with the ghosts of all the souls who'd depended on this precious tradition to ease their difficult lives.

As he had frequently the whole morning, he turned toward Susan to catch her watching him, her own eyes shining.

But her answering smile had him wondering how great his Naughty versus Nice balance must have been over the past year.

He'd surely done a whole hell of a lot of things right if whatever came next was anywhere near as great as the last few hours.

He walked toward her, letting the crowd move forward to gather around the tracks.

His often-annoying-but-still-fantastic buddy Billy had made it back in plenty of time to help keep anyone from getting too close before the train made its appearance. And to get in plenty of pointed looks at Paul, and a few unsubtle gestures encouraging him to get *closer* to Susan.

As if Paul hadn't already figured that part out for himself.

Right now, much as he already liked Chris and Will, he didn't mind one bit when they followed the crowd.

Leaving him and Susan more or less alone for the first time since they'd first spoken that morning.

The way the snow collected on the pink scarf that had first caught his attention and in her brown curls kept the cold from getting anywhere near him.

"I don't know how to thank you, Paul," she said, head lowered and looking up at him. "This couldn't have gone any better even without all the surprises."

"I'd say they were more good surprises than bad, at least from my perspective. Listen, being part of all this is thanks enough. But I have an idea if you're looking for suggestions."

Susan raised her chin and stepped closer.

"After I got over the initial shock of seeing nothing but a sea of canvas, I'd say the unexpected turned out to be flat-out wonderful. And yes, I'd love to hear your ideas, since I've got a couple of my own."

The train whistle sounded again, much closer, and now Paul heard the metal-on-metal song of the rails ringing out. A sound he'd loved his whole life long, enough to spend his working years both chasing it and making sure it continued.

And it all faded into the background as he gazed into Susan's eyes.

"Once everything's wrapped up for the day here," he said, "want to have lunch with me? Your favorite place in town, or anywhere else. As long as we can sit still and talk, spend some time getting to know each other."

She reached out and took his hand, lighting up every part of him with her warm fingers.

"That sounds great to me. I'd suggest the Railsong Café right across the street. They have all kinds of specials for the day. And quiet corners for a bit of privacy."

The crowd erupted into cheers perfectly timed with Paul's heart.

He and Susan exchanged a grin, and both turned to see the sleek green train rolling slowly into view. Several passenger cars rolled by, all with volunteers dressed like Santa's elves waving out the windows.

Then the star of the show appeared as the train came to a halt. The Santa man himself in all his red-suited, white-bearded glory—standing at the back of a specially made caboose decorated with wreaths and garlands and strings of blinking lights.

And a small army of those modern-day elves swarmed out through the fairy-tale-perfect, light and graceful fall of snow, arms full of gifts and faces wreathed with smiles.

Paul turned back to Susan, wondering at the gift that hadn't even crossed his mind when he got up that morning, now holding his hand and standing close enough to kiss.

"The Railsong Café it is," he said. "And I can't wait to find out what happens next."

Even with the excited crowd noise and chuff of a locomotive settling into a stop, Paul heard Susan's deep and sexy laugh.

"I have at *least* one idea of my own about that."

She closed the distance between them, and her lips met his.

In that warm sweetness, Paul finally understood what all those romance stories were talking about.

And he couldn't wait to get started living out the one he and Susan had just begun.

ELLAJANE CLOSE HER eyes and smiled, letting the cheers and chorus of *awwww* wash over and through her. Letting her body and mind drift away from the magical snowfall starting in one charming Appalachian town, and into the pleasantly warm and tired sensation in her body from spending the day outside playing in another.

Letting her reality catch up with where her imagination —combined in seamless fluidity with Chris's—had taken all of them.

As she'd had no doubt she would, the first thing she saw was the light in his green eyes answering the delicious dance in her belly, like all those snowflakes in Estonoa and Lightning Gap combined and in motion together.

On one of the leather loveseats close to the fire, a pink-jammied Adam leaned over and smooched Kay on the cheek.

"Reminds me of how I felt when I first got you to hold still long enough to lay a good one on you," he said.

Kay laughed, and that broad smile surely hadn't changed in all the years they'd been together.

"Well, I knew that was what you had in your mind, Adam. *And* that I'd be a goner as soon as you got hold of me. That's why I avoided you just as long as I could."

Mr. Seagon reached over and took his wife's hand, and they shared the fond smile of all their decades together.

"We might have to tell you the story of how we met right

here in this very basement someday," he said. "Or even better, see if EllaJane and Chris want to help us turn it into one of their wonderful stories."

Chris leaned close enough to touch shoulders with Ella-Jane, and she leaned right back with a sigh.

"I'd sure love to hear it," Chris said. "If anyone could bring it to life for the rest of us, EllaJane could."

She leaned her head against his for a quick second, already wishing for more.

"If you decide to share, the two of us will do our best to do it justice."

Ivy leaned over to scratch BeeGirl's ears, who promptly stretched her back and all four legs, sending all the metal bits on their goofy matching sweaters reflecting the firelight.

"Well, all I know is love and companionship come and go, if you're lucky enough to keep finding it. But the one thing I've learned to rely on is the sweetness at the heart of a good hound dog. That, good storytelling, and a few damn fine friends. Ready to head across the street?"

"Coming right along, you grouchy old fool." Venus got to her feet and stretched, and everyone else moved with her. "I get the feeling all of us are going to have a fabulous night after that wonderful story."

Only EllaJane and Chris stayed where they were, only steps away from their apartments and sleep.

Or whatever else the night might bring.

"How about it, Chris?" EllaJane said, moving away just enough so she could see his eyes. "Think we've got what it takes to write a great romance?"

"I'm starting to think it would be a real shame if we don't." Then his brow creased. "But maybe, after a story like that..."

EllaJane nodded, not loving what she was had to say next.

"Yeah, I read a lot about that this morning. I found the records from other writers and characters, almost like—"

"Diaries," they both said at the same instant.

EllaJane laughed, surprised at a delightful wave of relief.

"You found those too? I thought I was the only one sneaking around that early."

Chris glanced around the now-empty room.

"You were. I was in the grips of my night owl ways even more than usual last night. I'm guessing we both read about the way parts of a good story can...carry over? The *feel* of it?"

"I did read that," Ella Jane said. "Makes sense with the way we work, you know? So I think you're right, at least for now. Because later on, things might change."

Chris leaned closer and smiled, and EllaJane was quite sure he felt the same way she did, sweet romance story or not.

"Things might just change for the better. And that will be worth the wait."

KARI KILGORE

AUTHOR OF SONGS IN THE MOUNTAIN AND SOUL DEEP

A Current Made of Joy

A VOICES THROUGH TIME STORY

For everyone who finds their true companion
who makes them more themselves

A CURRENT MADE OF JOY

THE FOURTH DAY of the Odds and Endings bookstore's Mid-Holiday Madness storytelling week dawned bitterly cold, preserving the lovely snowfall of the day before and the fanciful structures all the residents of Lighting Gap, Virginia, had created.

Everyone could still peek out the windows of the charming shops and restaurants tucked into the grand Victorian houses along Lightning Rock Road without having to get into the fierce wind. The collections of multicolored snow families were only a little bit worse for wear, losing a few of their edges and maybe a loose bit or two of their fancy party clothes.

The snow forts lingered sturdy and solid, and the few folks who did venture outside couldn't help smiling at the odd music of that wind dancing through all the tunnels and passageways.

The giant coffee cup in front of Kay's Café had held up beautifully, and Kay herself made sure to stay open despite the lack of her usual stream of customers. She reasoned that anyone who *did* brave the chill would need coffee or tea, cider or hot cocoa more than ever.

Between weariness from all those hours adult and children alike had dedicated to playing the day before and temperatures dipping perilously close to zero, the entire town agreed on a day of rest without a word being said. A common enough occurrence during the strange in-between week that falls between Christmas and New Year's Eve, to be sure.

And of course with the peculiar magic of Lightning Gap and especially the Odds and Endings bookstore, even a day best left to relaxation would likely bring something unusual.

Inside the glorious purple Victorian house that held Odds and Endings—and remarkably welcoming and peaceful shelter for the four people who currently lived there —that meant hours spent puttering around the countless shelves in the three upstairs stories, then hours more spent curling up to read.

The wonderful aroma of Carabelle Seagon's Earl Grey tea filled the house from top to bottom, the perfect compliment to the delightful scent of books from nearly every possible era tucked onto gleaming wooden shelves.

She and her husband Arthur had owned the bookstore for longer than anyone could remember, and their bright personalities added as much to a visit as the dizzying array of books. Arthur's lighter-than-air and amazingly crisp ginger cookies gave the tea and the peaceful day just the right amount of spice.

Chris Ramsey had spent the day immersed in a fantastic collection of comic books and graphic novels in a sprawling room on the second floor, the walls decorated with a kaleidoscope of covers from the ones too far past their prime to save. Giving himself the gift of escape from the kind of storytelling he'd been sharing with the closest members of the Odds and Endings family over the past few days.

He might be discovering his own previously unknown ability to spin a yarn, but since he couldn't manage to draw a circle or square without help, he had no plans to venture over to the visual side.

The last several weeks working with EllaJane Cole, the current writer-in-residence at the bookstore, had given him more thrills, chills, and excitement than all the ink and adventures surrounding him put together.

Because Chris hadn't only been reading or listening to the stories, much as he enjoyed that part of their collaboration.

He'd been *living* the stories. Serving as EllaJane's character and helping her create the words and worlds and adventures. At night when he slept, often during the day when the two of them worked together in a half-dreaming trance.

Chris had learned the incredible magic of becoming a bridge. A conduit between EllaJane's fingers on the keyboard and the mysterious reservoir of stories and imagination.

After years of hoping he'd get the chance, the reality rocketed light years past everything he'd imagined.

The biggest part that had never even crossed his mind until this week was taking a turn as a storyteller himself. He wasn't only gathering on remarkably comfortable brown leather sofas and chairs with the closest members of the Odds and Endings family to listen, wonderful as that was. All of them cozy and snug in front of a thriving fire in the fabulous hidden basement full of books too beloved and rare to keep in the public part of the bookstore.

Chris had actually told the tale himself once, stepping out of his own world and bringing a brand new one to life.

He'd do the same tonight, assuming he didn't manage to

get in his own way instead of letting the characters create the magic.

The same tight-knit group with an insatiable passion for stories sat around him now, all properly warmed by cider, tea, and even cups of scratch-made eggnog. Each and every one gussied up with a healthy dose of the Seagons' seemingly endless supply of fine bourbon.

Kay and her husband Adam had supplied the surprise eggnog after spending part of their day tinkering with the recipe and preparation. As was often the case, neither one of them would reveal their secret. And everyone who tasted the smooth, rich concoction honestly declared it the best they'd ever had.

Tonight the two of them wore matching old-fashioned long flannel underwear, covering them from head to toe in a field of red and white and green candy canes. Soft black booties gave the impression that they'd just hurried inside from tending to some kind of chore that had to be done, but wasn't worth putting on real clothing for.

On the sofa across from Chris and EllaJane, Ivy Gweddon and Venus Mullins perched, with Ivy's delightful redbone hound BeeGirl sprawled between them. All three of them were outfitted in honest-to-goodness nightshirts; the same kind often depicted in illustrations of *T'was the Night Before Christmas*.

But these weren't the typical white cotton versions, and no one who'd ever spent any time with Venus would have believed she could possibly own anything so ordinary.

Hers was a shimmering black fabric that moved like water, somehow reflecting every color in the rainbow. Ivy's was a deep russet orange, accented with black piping. A much-appreciated gift from Venus, especially since a perfectly fitted version for BeeGirl had been included in the package.

The Seagons held court in their matching leather chairs

near the fire, both wearing their usual sweatpants and shirt. But these might have been more suited for the upcoming Valentine's Day parties than New Year's Eve, since they were covered in hearts of every shape and hue.

Chis couldn't pretend the hearts and all the matching outfits might not be a comment on the growing flirtation, curiosity, attraction, whatever you wanted to call it, between himself and EllaJane.

Tonight she'd come out of her basement apartment in an absurdly warm-looking navy blue...not quite nightgown, but more than a tunic. The thick, fuzzy fabric covered her from neck to wrists to ankles, sweeping just over the floor as she walked.

When she curled up on the sofa beside Chris, he'd spotted the vivid pink tights she wore underneath, as if she was heading to a dance recital afterwards.

For his part, he'd reverted to his reliable, comfortable black sweatpants and dark-gray shirt. But he'd made a point of adding sunshine-yellow fuzzy socks to go with a royal-purple sweater.

If he couldn't liven up his look here, in the secret basement with people who'd heard him spin his first yarn, he'd never make the leap anywhere.

A vividly colorful leap he'd seen in what EllaJane wore on her habitual late-night wanderings through the bookstore.

Rather than standing to make her own introduction, Carabelle Seagon stayed put, larger-than-usual mug of eggnog in hand. Chris didn't have to glance at his watch to know the magic of eleven past the hour had arrived. The musical lilt of her mountain accent made him smile, as always.

"We surely all know each other well enough for me to let Chris introduce his story. All I'll say is I can't wait to see which of our mystery writer's worlds he walks us through this evening. And that I've thoroughly enjoyed hearing stories from places and characters I know so well. I have no doubt our author will be thrilled."

Both Chris and EllaJane had been unable to resist writing in various worlds from one of their fellow Odds and Endings authors, certainly not once they realized they had the same favorite. They'd worked together to pick out books for everyone that fit their selections, neatly wrapped in plain brown paper under the fabulous tree in the corner of the basement.

He paused for a few seconds, though he suspected trying to gather his thoughts before he jumped into either side of storytelling was futile.

Thoughts, especially those of the logical or emotional kind, could only cause him trouble.

"All of you know I'm fairly new to creating stories, much less introducing them. Today and tonight, I've had the chance to really learn something I've heard writers say my whole life. The best way to tell the tale is to get out of your own way." He smiled at everyone in turn. Except BeeGirl, who was sprawled on her back and gently snoring.

"Tonight we have a tale of discovery. Of connection and reconnection, and of all the ways a bit of magical power can change lives. Ways even the people who hold that power never expected."

He looked into EllaJane's eyes for a second, remembering how reasonable it seemed the night before when they'd agreed not to act on the growing attraction between them. How their idea of resisting each other—paying heed to worries about a romantic story driving their feelings—had somehow made perfect sense.

But looking at her right now, he was quite sure they'd been playing a fool's game.

One that couldn't last much longer. Because no matter

how many different ways he'd tried to direct his story onto a different topic, a different path, a different feel, the characters simply laughed and made it clear they were going to keep right on with what they wanted to do.

Sinking into the near-trace he shared with EllaJane could only put him more firmly in the character's control. And maybe that was the best thing for everyone.

Chris closed his eyes and drifted away, letting the warm currents of imagination and connection sweep him into another time, place, and point of view.

And he began the tale.

OUT OF ALL THE places he'd been lucky enough to spend holidays as a kid, Mark Hersch loved back home in Bountyfield, Virginia, the most.

His father's Air Force career took them all around the country and the world on grand adventures full of unforgettable experiences. Years spent in Germany, traveling around the rest of Europe every chance they got. Visits to England and Italy for Christmas and New Year's, and the odd dislocation of what he'd always known as cold-weather holidays in the heat of mid-summer Australia.

He'd been fortunate enough to see fireworks in Paris, watch people spin huge balls of fire for Hogmanay in Scotland, and visit holiday markets in Austria. They'd even spent one unforgettable night watching the ball drop in Times Square in Manhattan, part of a crush of noise and people and too much excitement that he didn't need to do twice.

Grateful as he was for all those memories, Mark had always loved the rare years he and his parents instead traveled back to the Appalachian Mountains. Taking their chance to settle in for a quiet, family-filled Christmas at home with Mark's grandparents.

Simple pleasures like helping decorate a tree freshly harvested from the same land where generations before had collected theirs. Stuffing himself silly on his Granny's chocolate and peanut butter fudge, and his Papaw's rather potent rum balls.

Gathering around the fireplace to read or listen to his grandparents spin their own memories, once or twice while a postcard-perfect snowfall transformed the world all around them into a magical snow globe landscape.

Without a trace of the excitement of holidays in a big city, sure, or the constant surprise and disorientation of celebrations in another culture. Things his parents both thrived on and still missed years after they'd finally left the Air Force way of life. Enough that they usually picked somewhere exciting for a mid-winter escape to this day.

Mark's strong desire to get back to the mountains was one of the many reasons he and his parents hadn't quite understood each other, then or now.

And out of all of those times—including his many visits since moving himself to Richmond more than ten years back —none had delighted him so much as this one.

Rather than traveling to wherever his parents had gotten off to this year, or else hanging out in his unremarkable bachelor's apartment, Mark was back in Hartstown.

Spending his first Christmas Eve with the woman he'd only met a few weeks before. But the intensity of their underground adventure together and the days since already had Mark hoping he'd be right by her side for all the holidays to come.

Beth Azen's living room started out cozy and welcoming, with colorful old-fashioned braided rag rugs over the century-old mellow hardwood floors. Enlarged black-and-white historical photos shared wall space with modern art prints and gorgeous photographs she'd taken herself.

The pattern continued with an antique wooden rocking chair draped with a well-worn and loved flowery quilt alongside deep-cushioned sofas and chairs in muted earth tones. Perfect for cuddling, whether that was Mark with Beth, or her sweet Redbone hound dog Janie with one or both of them.

A not-yet-decorated Virginia pine tree sat in the corner with several cardboard boxes tucked underneath. Most Beth said were full of her usual ornaments and lights and garlands and such, and a few Mark had carried in through the snow when he arrived that afternoon. Setting up a tree in his empty apartment back in Richmond had hardly seemed worth the trouble when he was delighted to be staying put in the mountains until the new year.

He kept to himself how sentimental and lovestruck he felt at the idea of adding his collection of inherited ornaments and offbeat additions to hers on the same tree.

Right now the homey scent of a good fire in Beth's woodstove was enhanced by the comfort-food-goodness of Mark's best-received cooking effort since he'd moved out on his own years ago. A big bowl of chili over brown rice, spicy enough to warm everyone through and through, but not enough to stir up heartburn.

Beth had enough of that right now, brought on by the painkillers she was taking for her broken arm.

The one she'd broken saving his life in an old, abandoned house-pit coal mine a few weeks ago, barely an hour after she'd kissed him for the first time.

Mark alternated between feeling guilty, awestruck, and proud of the way she'd shoved him out of the way, protecting him from a falling rock that surely would have cracked his skull as neatly as it had her arm.

All because her connection with the lively spectral world around Hartstown had given her a split-second warning that a troublesome and ornery ghost was about to drop a good-sized chunk of the roof on his head.

He'd arranged her rolling laptop desk so she could sit by the fire and eat, using her left hand without having too much trouble. Of course her dominant right arm was the injured one, though she hid her frustration well.

So she curled up at the end of one of her wonderful sofas, curly brown hair allowed to fend for itself, leaving it nearly as unpredictable and free as Mark's strawberry blond mop. Wearing her current uniform of dark sweatpants and matching wool socks, with a pair of purple Birkenstocks close by for easy on and off.

Today she'd swiped his burgundy-faded-nearly-to-pink Virginia Tech t-shirt out of his bag for herself. He had no trouble at all admitting how much better the shirt looked on her than it ever had on him.

Beth turned to him and smiled, her blue eyes reflecting the firelight and what he hoped was satisfaction. Or at least an acceptable reduction of hunger.

The rapidly emptied bowl on the tray was a good hint.

"This is absolutely *delicious*, Mark. Any chance you'll share the recipe once I'm able to return the favor and make it for you?"

Mark made a show of considering his options carefully. Pursing his lips, tilting his head to one side. He even laid it on thick enough to scratch his beard for a second.

Janie put a stop to his nonsense with an exaggerated, drawn-out inhale and even longer grumbling sigh from her flannel dog bed near the wood stove.

"I suppose I could be convinced to part with my secrets," Mark said through laughter. "No way I could refuse Janie."

"She does all my negotiating for that exact reason. Listen,

I know you had a long drive today. We don't have to bother with the tree tonight after you cooked and all."

Mark set his own empty bowl aside and scooted close enough to carefully put his arm around her.

"You don't really expect me to leave your tree unfinished on Christmas Eve, do you? I've got some of my grandparents' decorations packed up right over there, just waiting for their turn in the spotlight. They'd come back to haunt me for sure if I failed in this very reasonable duty."

Beth snorted and rolled her eyes.

"Do you really think *you'd* know about a haunting around here before I did? You forget I seem to have become the resident expert, at least on this side of the veil."

"Well no, I didn't exactly forget. I'm just getting used to the idea is all. Believe it or not, so far you're the only person I know with a radio station in your mind tuned in to the after-life. How are they this evening?"

"Turns out Christmas Eve is all singing, all the time. Much quieter than they were before, when I first heard them. I wish they were louder for a change, to tell you the truth, instead of sounding like a tinny old radio in another room. I have to concentrate hard enough to give myself a headache to hear anyone talk. When she can get through, Clina tells me they'll keep this up right through Old Christmas Eve on January sixth, too."

She raised her eyebrows, but she smiled.

"It's kind of nice, hearing some of these old hymns again. My family who sang those passed a long time ago."

Clina was the main connection to the ethereal world, the first one to reach out to Beth, after years of trying to warn someone in the land of the living about the ghost trapped in the old mine. Other spirits spoke up in the background, but they most often made themselves known by their songs.

Mark and Beth both suspected Clina's feisty and

outspoken ways, and her pure stubbornness, had given her the advantage when it came to getting through to someone still living and breathing.

Mark had only heard those voices on that dreadful, scary, amazing day. He hoped the gift he had tucked away with his holiday decorations might turn up the signal for him and for Beth.

He had folks he'd dearly love to speak to again, and he was sure she did too.

Neither of them was willing to consider what might happen if word of her odd connection ever got out to the general population.

"In that case," he said, kissing her cheek before he stood and gathered up their bowls, "sounds like this is the perfect time to get the tree all dressed up and ready for tomorrow. I'm not any kind of a singer, but I'll do my best. My guess is Janie will beg me to stop before you do."

Thankfully Beth opted for one of her own holiday-themed playlists, sparing Mark the sting of inevitable canine disapproval.

He wasn't the least bit surprised to hear everything from a classic recording of *The Nutcracker Suite* to *A Charlie Brown Christmas* to mellow, jazzy versions of old standards. Loretta Lynn, Elvis Presley, and Dolly Parton scattered throughout brought home their shared Southern and mountain roots, since he knew the words to every one whether he sang out loud or not.

After an hour or so of good-natured tree trimming, punctuated with a respectable amount of laughter and tales about the origins of various decorations, the ordinary pine was transformed into a wonderfully cheery Christmas tree.

The combination of brand-new color-changing lights reflecting off of old-fashioned silver garland played especially well with the mix of modern matte globes and spires alongside bright, extra-shiny glass ornaments. Several of those were well older than Mark, and a few stretched past his thirty-six years and into six decades or more.

The ones that made him smile the most were the hand-painted ones he and Beth both had carried around since their grade-school years. Little ceramic elves, wrapped presents, and tiny trees, covered with kid-sized splatters and drops that made them all the more precious. Those and enough photos of both of them from their awkward (and in her case, adorable) younger years made Mark feel like they'd known each other much longer than a few incredible weeks.

Beth sat back from where they'd knelt side-by-side, arranging the quilted tree skirt Mark's Granny made for him the year he was born. She'd done the same for all his cousins, using old clothing she'd saved back from her own children's growing up years, creating wonderful combinations of colors, shapes, and textures.

Something about Beth's face in the firelight as she brushed back her hair struck Mark, opening the space she'd taken up in his heart a good bit deeper. He couldn't yet do everything he wanted to for her, mainly because he'd need as many years as he could manage for most of it.

But he found he couldn't wait one more second to give her the present he was most excited about. The others he had stashed in the car and no doubt Beth had somewhere in the house could wait until they woke in the morning.

Not only was this one perfect for her, but he'd never imagined such a thing could exist until he met her.

He reached into the last cardboard box, labeled "Holiday Stuff" in his own neat handwriting. Only one thing was left inside besides the piles of packing paper and bubble wrap he'd used for all those years to keep everything safe.

A simple red velvet drawstring bag with a black jewelry box inside, a good bit bigger than one for a ring.

"I meant to wait until tomorrow for this," he said. "But this seems like the perfect time. And the truth is I've used up pretty much all my patience waiting to see how you like it."

Beth carefully shifted until she sat cross-legged, which prompted Janie to amble over and settle her head in Beth's lap with another of her voluminous sighs.

Beth had made it clear almost from the first second they left the hospital with her arm in a cast that she wanted to do as much as possible for herself, thank you very much.

But Mark did make sure the string was untied before he handed it over.

"Don't worry," he said, leaning forward to scratch Janie's long, red ears. "I've got a few things for Janie, too."

"Good thing. Otherwise she'll send you right back out into the snow after something, stores closed or not. Is this… Never mind. You're going to tell me to stop asking questions already and just open it."

"You got it."

Mark grinned and moved until he sat cross-legged in front of Beth, their knees touching. Giddy as a little boy on Christmas morning, but in reverse.

He couldn't remember ever being as excited to *get* a present as he was to *give* this one.

With impressive dexterity between her restricted right hand and her free left one, Beth opened the jewelry box while staring into his eyes.

Then she looked down and gasped.

Inside was an irregular bit of glass a little bigger than Mark's thumbnail. The last remnant of the rectangular glass-plate photographic negative that Clina had used to get through to Beth. She and Mark had returned from rescuing their ghost miner to find it shattered but untouched, all the pieces in exactly the same spot on the front seat of a pickup truck.

The incredibly clear black-and-white image showed Clina's face, her dark hair, and a huge white hat tilted at a jaunty angle. Probably the only photo of her remaining in the world, from an age when each photograph was a precious thing. Long before everyone carried thousands of them around in their pockets.

A buddy of Mark's back in Richmond had smoothed the jagged edges, sealed the whole thing, then coated the outside with copper. The sparkling pendant now hung from a copper necklace that gleamed with the changing lights on the Christmas tree.

Beth's face lit in a gorgeous smile that sent Mark's heart soaring.

"It's just *perfect*, Mark," she said, her voice breathy and low. "I can't imagine anything that could possibly make it better."

He returned her smile and leaned forward.

"I can. I've been counting the minutes to see you wearing this since I got it."

She laughed, and he was startled and pleased to see tears in her lovely blue eyes. She leaned forward herself and met him in a long, luxurious kiss.

"Then by all means, please do the honors."

Mark pulled the necklace free and moved behind her, one hand on her shoulder. He took the irresistible opportunity to kiss the soft skin of her neck just under her hairline, breathing in her scent that already felt like home.

The chain was long enough that she'd be able to put it on without using the clasp, but he opened it anyway. When the glass touched her chest not far above her heart, she drew in a sharp breath.

"I can hear them loud and clear as before we went into that house pit, when I had the whole glass-plate negative," she whispered, covering the bit of glass with her hand. By the time Mark got back around so he could see her face, she laughed. "I didn't realize how much I'd missed all of you until right this second."

She let go and grabbed Mark's hand, and he had the eerie sensation of a radio station snapping into tune inside his mind. Clina Jane herself was a quarrelling up a storm, as his own Papaw would have said, but Mark didn't miss the happiness and lilt in her thick mountain accent.

"...reckoned you might scratch out a little bit of time to say hello one of these long days or nights. That feller of yours must be a right good one to keep you so caught up as to forget all about the rest of us."

Beth raised Mark's hand to her lips, then held his palm over her necklace. The disorderly teenage boy inside of him couldn't resist pointing out the soft curve of her breasts under his old t-shirt.

"He *is* a right good feller," Beth said. "Mark is the one who got this necklace made so we can talk a lot easier now. But I'm not afraid to tell you I'll take it off on purpose from time to time, so I can get a bit of peace and quiet." The suggestive look in her eyes got Mark's rowdy inner teenager perking up even more. "And some privacy."

Several voices chuckled along with Clina, and Mark felt his cheeks turn red right along with Beth's.

"Well I should surely hope you do just that," Clina said. "Every chance you can *while* you can is what I say. If you think you might see your way to hold off for a spell, got someone here who sure does want to talk to you."

"Talk to me?" Beth said. "Or to Mark?"

Mark could hear the rise and fall of someone else talking, but he couldn't make out any of the words. Almost as if Clina stood in the middle of a huge cocktail party where moonshine was the preferred libation rather than wine.

"This one's wanting to speak to Mark," Clina said, and

now she sounded puzzled. "Already trying to just now, but seems like you can't hear."

Beth frowned. "I heard, Clina, but kind of quiet. Something about... Well, it doesn't make sense to worry about any of this sounding strange at this point. Something about a bug?"

This time Mark gasped, and his heart jumped up and paid close attention.

"Was it..." He stopped, forcing himself to slow down and not get too agitated. "Did he say water bug, Beth?"

"That's *exactly* what he said. I thought I misunderstood. Kind of a raspy voice?"

A breathless laugh escaped Mark, and he found himself blinking back tears. He glanced toward the tree, where a metal ornament shaped like a holly wreath the size of his pre-growth-spurt fifteen-year-old hand nestled among the pine needles. Framing a still-bright color photo of himself and his Papaw, grinning with their cheeks together.

"Yeah, from all his rough living years, he used to say. Is that my *grandfather*, Clina? Walt Hersch?"

This time the voice on the other side was louder, but Mark still couldn't make out the words. But he could tell whoever was talking was as excited—and frustrated—as he was.

Clina sounded very much the same.

"This here is Walt standing close by my side, can't work out why you ain't hearing him same as me. You picking up on him, Beth?"

Beth slipped the bit of glass into Mark's hand, then covered it with her own.

"I hear him, but I only catch every few words. Like we're on a bad connection, or it keeps shorting out. I don't suppose you have any ideas how to clear it up over there?"

Clina let out a sharp exclamation not unlike his Granny

use to make, often at his Papaw, but enough times toward Mark that he understood what Clina meant.

Not quite a word, but the closest he could get to explaining it was a longer, more enunciated version of shooing away some kind of animal.

More like *shew*.

"Now how exactly is it you think *I* could tell *you* that?" Clina said. "You're the ones that know what made the difference in the first place. I expect you might could do something else along the same lines."

Mark laughed under his breath, feeling exactly like the little boy, or grown man, who'd earned such an exasperated response. Beth's raised eyebrows and slow head shake let him know she understood just fine herself.

"All I know is we have something that's connected to you," Beth said. "From what you told me the first day I heard you, there's a good chance you held the same glass plate negative in your hand at some point. But it... I don't know, put you into my mind? Maybe that opened up the channel between us?"

Mark grunted, caught up in the uncomfortable certainty that he was missing something obvious. So much so that he'd be annoyed with himself once he finally caught hold of it.

"You're saying this connection might be like opening a new channel for water," he said, thinking out loud to try to clear up his own connections. "Once you show it the way to go and keep it open, that passage only gets stronger."

Much as he didn't want to, he shifted away from Beth and let his mind relax while his gaze wandered the room. From the woodstove that would soon need feeding, to the laptop table by the couch where he'd so happily fed Beth. Janie's snores made it clear she had a pleasantly full belly, and he had a healthy supply of holiday dog treats in the trunk of his car to make sure she stayed that way while he was here.

A lot like his Granny and Papaw always did any time he visited, but especially over the holidays.

The *holidays*...

Mark shifted onto his knees and plucked the wreath ornament with the photo of himself and his Papaw down from the tree. The metal was cool and prickly against his fingers.

"I wonder if something like this might do the trick," he said, settling back beside Beth.

Her eyes lit up and she grinned.

"Makes sense to me, since you made it and it hung on your grandparents' tree for so long. Here."

She put one of his hands over the necklace again, then wrapped her fingers around the hand holding the ornament.

"Okay, Clina, have Mark's Papaw try to talk again. Tell him we're holding on to a picture of him and Mark together, inside a Christmas wreath."

Mark heard a quick burst of words, then Clina spoke clearly again.

"Well that got Walt right perked up and grinning like a fool. Reckon it might work."

For a few seconds, Mark was afraid they'd be stuck with the tantalizing hint of sound without words. He heard the beloved rise and fall, the slow cadence he remembered from all the nights when their shared trait of insomnia led to long conversations between him and his Papaw.

But only that. No words.

"Think about that channel, Mark," Beth said, leaning her forehead against his. "Where the water wants to go once you show it how."

Mark closed his eyes and remembered all the ways he'd managed to manipulate water when he was a kid. At the beach, kneeling close to the waves, moving as the tide gradually took out his series of sand dams and canals. But not until he'd figured out how to make it bend to his will, at least for a little while.

Here in the mountains during a good hard rain, pushing around the leaves and rocks to make the streams and creeks flow the way he wanted them to.

And of course in mud puddles whenever he got away from whoever was supposed to be minding him. Only his Papaw had understood that one, and joined in the game.

Turning Mark into Water Bug, and his Papaw into Mud Bug.

Mark made those same adjustments now. Digging out a bit here, building up a bit there.

Pushing something jamming up the middle to one side so the flow could finally break through.

And the sound slowly resolved itself.

Turning into a voice...raspy with all those hard-living years.

Then tuning in a tiny bit at a time, fading and returning, much more like an old knob radio than anything resembling digital.

Finally hitting the sweet spot and coming in loud and clear.

"...hear me, Mark? I'll just keep right on a-talking 'til you work it out like you always do."

Mark drew in a slow, shuddering breath and opened his eyes, looking right into Beth's.

He felt like that warm ocean water inside and out now.

But the current was entirely made of joy.

"I'm right here, Mud Bug. It's been about half my life too long since I heard your voice."

"I can't even begin to tell you how much I missed you, Water Bug. Never did think I'd get to speak to you before your own time way on off into the future. Beth, I sure am awful pleased to speak to you."

"I'm glad to make your acquaintance too, Mr. Hersch. Walt. You've got a mighty fine grandson here."

Beth sat back, but she kept hold of the ornament and Mark's hand.

"I surely do," Mark's Papaw said. "Hope we don't wear out our welcome with all these years of catching up to do."

"Hang on," Mark said. "Let me see how we might be able to manage that." He moved the ornament away, setting it on his Granny's tree skirt quilt. "Still good?"

"Right here."

Mark worked through several changes, testing the result each time. Letting go of the necklace, but still touching Beth. Trying the necklace on himself. Holding the ornament.

In the end, the only thing that worked was touching Beth while she wore the necklace, or holding it in his own hand while touching her. They left the ornament on the tree —its vital service as the initial conduit fulfilled—and moved back to the sofa with Janie arranging herself with her head in Mark's lap this time.

"I think we can work out some kind of schedule," Beth said. "Maybe when I'm concentrating on something else. Or half-asleep."

"Which I think you are right now, from the way your eyes look," Mark said. "I just have one more question, then I'm afraid we're going to have to sign off for the night. Do you know where Granny is, Papaw? Is she there with you?"

The silence stretched on long enough for Mark to worry about losing the ethereal connection, but he could still hear that radio-station hum. Almost like he'd tuned in to a living thing.

"I'm right sorry to have to say this to you, Mark, but I haven't seen her here. I surely would like to."

"We never can tell who will bring themselves to this place," Clina said. "Sometimes it takes a right long time.

Knowing how to talk to the living might make a difference in the end."

Mark kissed Beth's cheek again, already dreading having to head back to Richmond when January second rolled around. Being away from her for days was bad enough, let alone weeks.

He'd only known her for a tiny fraction of the time his grandparents had been together, but already he couldn't stand to imagine spending an eternity without her.

"I hope she shows up soon, Papaw," he said. "And I couldn't be happier to be able to talk to you. Want to see what we can't get into tomorrow?"

"Wouldn't miss it for this world or yours, Water Bug."

Beth started to lift the necklace over her head, but Mark held it for one incredibly important thing he'd almost over-looked. A lapse that would had gotten him his Granny's annoyed *shew* for certain.

"I don't know how I could possibly thank you enough, Clina," he said. "So I'll just say please let me know if there's anything I can do for you or anyone else there. Or anyone on this side."

Clina's spoke in a much softer voice than he'd heard from her before.

"I'm right glad to be able to do it, Mark. You and Beth there have livened up our side of the veil considerably, and we made a great change for all of us living and passed on by bringing that lost coal miner's soul up out of the ground. Don't you worry one bit. You'll be hearing from me for sure."

Mark slipped the necklace away, the glass and copper catching the multicolored light from the Christmas tree, and put it gently back into its box.

He and Beth stared at each other, firelight and tree light playing over the whole scene, for longer than he thought either one of them would be able to hold out. Mark was starting to think he'd either drown or pass out cold in the rising tides of delight, gratitude, and awe fighting it out for control of his heart and mind.

Nothing he knew the words for felt equal to the task.

Then Janie's groaning stretch broke the quiet before either one of them had to.

"I can still hear them," Beth said, touching the spot on her chest where the necklace had been. "Not quite as loud, but better than I could before. It really is like the way got cleared by what you did."

"What we *both* did. There's so many things about where I am right now that I never would have imagined a month ago. But having the chance to speak to my Papaw again... That one never would have even occurred to me. Even more than with Clina, saying thank you doesn't begin to scratch the surface of how I feel right now."

Beth rolled her eyes and pushed at him with her shoulder.

"I'd say you can let yourself off the hook for that one, sweetheart. I'm more than happy to listen to you talk about how you feel, and I very much want to know more about your Papaw now that he's part of the radio station inside my head. But take figuring out how *you* should thank *me* for the gift you gave me off your list of worries."

Mark closed his eyes for a second, strangely relieved at her words. And feeling the long day of anticipation and driving and the snowstorm and the last half hour catching up to him all at once.

"Sounds great to me," he said. "Probably about time I let you and Janie get some sleep anyway."

Janie perked up fast enough to send her long ears flopping, and Beth blew a raspberry through her pursed lips.

"Oh yeah, we're the tired ones and you're all revved up and ready to go. Come on, then, let's all get settled in for the night. I'll even let you take Ms. Janie out to do her business if you don't mind."

At the words "do her business," Janie jumped down off the couch and shook herself from those luxurious red ears to her long, bushy tail, then trotted over to the door.

"I don't mind in the least." Mark stood, holding one arm out to Beth to hold until she stood beside him. "Walking around in a proper mountain snowstorm with a hound dog will do me a world of good. Especially if you help me warm up my cold feet later."

Beth laughed soft and low, pulling him closer with her good arm and gripping the front of his shirt with her other hand.

"If you think you can stay awake a little while longer," she said close against his ear, "I'll warm every last bit of you up. Inside and out."

An entirely different sort of thrill took Mark over, and he leaned in to kiss her good and long and proper.

"Oh, I'll stay awake, I can promise you that. And I'll do my best to encourage Janie to make her business quick."

Chris kept his eyes closed for several seconds, enjoying the chuckles not all that different from what he'd just heard from Beth inside his mind.

The aroma of bourbon and tea in the basement gradually replaced spicy chili in a cozy living room, but the fire and the pleasing scent of a good, clean hound dog stayed the same. When he finally opened his eyes, he was happy to see BeeGirl sitting up between Ivy and Venus, fully alert, long red ears up, and staring right at him.

She gave herself a good shake in her nightshirt, then let out a mighty sneeze.

"Now there's a heck of an endorsement for you," Ivy said over the much louder laughter. She scrubbed BeeGirl's neck and back. "Not only was she awake the whole time, but she felt the need to comment."

"I'll take that kind of expert comment in the spirit it was intended," Chris said. "And a sign that I got at least that part of the story right."

"You got a whole lot more than that right," Mr. Seagon said, beaming at Chris. "I think it's safe to say our first-ever story week with *two* folks telling the tales is heading toward what promises to be a very satisfying conclusion. Stories that begin in this basement have long had a way of working out exactly the way they're meant to, haven't they?"

He turned toward Mrs. Seagon, who promptly blushed and waved a hand toward him. But then she leaned over and gave him a resounding peck on the cheek.

"Much as I might like to argue," she said, "every word you just said is true. Thank you, Chris. I can't wait to hear what EllaJane has to share tomorrow night."

Mrs. Seagon smiled, picked up her now-empty eggnog mug, and headed toward the stairs.

"I suppose we should head back out as well," Kay said, smacking Adam on one candy cane covered leg. "The weather says much warmer tomorrow, so we'll have our hands full with people needing their comfort food to clean up after that storm."

As he had every other night during the flurry of motion and conversation, Chris turned to EllaJane. All the two of them had to do was turn out lights and head to their apartments only a few steps away. She grinned and nodded.

"That was wonderful, Chris. That's one of my favorite worlds to visit."

"Even though I didn't exactly avoid the romance story, despite trying to figure out how to do that all day long?"

She shrugged and held out both hands.

"Well, I didn't want to intrude today, but I did a bit more reading from the journals we talked about last night. The ones from our fellow writers and characters. It seems plenty of them believe it's not the story that drives the relationship, the mood. From what I saw today, neither of us could venture off into another genre even if we wanted to. And if we did, we might suffer…"

Chris laughed. "The dread and mythical writer's block?"

"That's what someone who's never written here might think. Hell, I'm sure you remember it's what I thought was happening my first couple of nights. I was afraid I'd be the first writer-in-residence to never get a word down during the entire year. But I've written more than I ever have before. Partly because I'm getting better at letting the characters and the story take the lead every single day."

They had the basement to themselves now, with only the glittering tree, the cozy fire, and thousands of books for company. Chris hesitated for a second, then held out his hand.

"So you're saying we might be better off letting the stories take the lead between us, too?"

EllaJane laced her fingers through his, and Chris wasn't sure if the massive storms said to rumble through Lightning Gap could come anywhere near the spark and shiver he felt at her touch.

"I'm saying I think the characters know more than we do, as usual. And maybe it's time we got out of the way, at least a little bit."

And his and EllaJane's first long and proper kiss flashed away any doubts about the time, the place, and the person being right.

KARI KILGORE

AUTHOR OF SONGS IN THE MOUNTAIN AND SOUL DEEP

Discovering Home

A Storms of Future Past Story

For everyone brave enough to seek their true family
and the families loving enough to welcome them

DISCOVERING HOME

When she settled in for the fifth evening of Mid-Holiday Madness at the Odds and Endings bookstore, EllaJane Cole was more weary than she'd been a couple of days ago after hours of sledding and snow forts and snowball fights.

She curled herself up on the couch nearest the fire, enjoying the ache and stretch in her muscles. One brought on by work rather than play, but work in Lightning Gap, Virginia, had a way of being almost as much fun.

The whole town had once again turned out for the cleanup of what had been the biggest winter storm for years. Wielding shovels and chainsaws, chains and handsaws. Clearing roads the big Felten County snowplows had skipped. Gathering up smaller branches after a huge, cantankerous crane truck hauled off a few massive trees that had succumbed to the glittering downfall.

The whole day turned into a wonderful chance for EllaJane to fill both her socializing quota and to overfill her writer's sensory and character reserves. She'd likely stored up enough to keep her inspired for all the rest of her residency and more.

Several of those fascinating locals gathered in the secret basement of the bookstore as they had for the past few days, all snug and toasty after putting their town back in order, eagerly awaiting a new story.

The comfortable fire that always at least smoldered in the big fireplace rose up high and fragrant, light and heat reflecting off the handmade tiles and filling the basement. The arrangement of wonderful brown leather chairs and sofas around the fire was anchored by a variety of antique wooden tables, each with barely enough space for a book and the liquid refreshment to go with it.

Tonight that refreshment came courtesy of Ivy Gweddon, a delightful mountain woman with a gruff, no-nonsense manner that concealed a fiercely loyal, kind-hearted warmth. One that came through loud and clear to anyone who saw Ivy with her adorable redbone hound BeeGirl.

She'd supplied a decadent elderberry wine made from her own bushes grown way up at the top of the Lightning Ridge that towered over and sheltered the town. Thick and sweet-tart, with earthy notes and a deceptive smoothness that covered up quite a kick.

EllaJane suspected *wine* might be a step or two down the distillation ladder from what she sipped from a glittering cut-crystal glass that highlighted the nearly black color, but she knew anyone lucky enough to taste it wouldn't dare report Ivy to the relevant authorities.

Of course if the relevant authorities in Lightning Gap were anything like the ones she knew back in Bountyfield, they probably cheerfully enjoyed Ivy's efforts and wouldn't dare get on her bad side.

Venus Mullins had passed around little medallions of rich chocolate brought back from her world travels, with a velvety sheen nearly as dark as the wine. EllaJane wasn't the only one who closed her eyes and sighed with every single nibble.

Not quite willing to give up their chance to share food with their friends, Kay and Adam had brought a cheese tray with them on their trek across the street from the lovely Victorian house that held Kay's Café. Not their normal focus on mountain comfort food by any means, and not likely to ever show up on the menu.

This was part of the special shipment Kay and Adam got in every year for their own private celebration.

Rich, creamy brie, cheddar sharp enough to make Ella-Jane's jaws ache, and soft bits of cheese that was stinky in the best possible way, all served with bits of hearty brown bread. It all paired exceptionally well with Ivy's wine and the Earl Grey tea the Seagons provided just in case.

For the first time in EllaJane's brief experience, the Seagons left their treasured bourbon upstairs in favor of the new decadent libation.

Tonight Mr. Seagon's rich brown sweatshirt was decorated with bunches of embroidered reindeer heads, all with shiny red noses that reflected the firelight. His matching pants showed reindeer feet and hooves, naturally. And even more naturally, Mrs. Seagon's purple version was decorated the same way, but her reindeer heads had mascara, lipstick, and earrings.

Kay and Adam sported pajamas made to look like wrapped presents in a dozen colors. And each of them wore a little toboggan hat with a red bow on top without a trace of self-consciousness. EllaJane's favorite part was the matching red bows on the toes of their green socks.

But the best outfit combination as far as she was concerned sat on the sofa across from her in the form of Ivy and Venus. They each wore what EllaJane thought of as granny nightgowns, with plenty of frills at the neck, wrists, and around the bottom of the skirt. No-nonsense Ivy's was sweet baby-doll-pink flannel, and they'd somehow found (or made) one of intense scarlet with sparkling bits of gold woven through for Venus.

The combination of fabric that would normally be found in an evening gown or possibly lingerie and the extremely conservative style was nothing short of delightful.

BeeGirl sat bundled up between them in a version covered in squirrels wearing Santa hats, which might have explained why she was wide awake rather than snoozing.

As for EllaJane herself, she'd opted for a decidedly old-fashioned cotton nightshirt her mother had made for her father, one she'd liberated from him when she'd gone off to college and never returned. The soft, well-worn fabric was covered in old cartoon characters, featuring a famous smart-tass bunny rabbit, clever road runner, and often hapless duck.

She had to turn the sleeves up several times, and the hem fell nearly to her ankles, and slipping it over her head felt like getting a big hug from both of them.

She had several reasons to smile at her writing partner Chris Ramsey tonight, not least because of what he'd unearthed from somewhere for the occasion. He wore his normal black sweatpants and charcoal-gray t-shirt, which along with various pairs of jeans EllaJane thought covered most of his wardrobe.

Until tonight.

He'd come strolling out of his apartment in an honest-to-goodness smoking jacket, one that would have been entirely appropriate during the Victorian Era when the house was built. The brilliant gold velvet with a brocade pattern practi-cally begged to be touched. The deep green lapels and accents added the perfect coordinating touch, especially since his slippers were of the same fabric and colors.

Even the mellow gleam of huge, textured silver buttons looked just right.

EllaJane had found herself wishing more and more

throughout the day that the two of them hadn't retired to their separate apartments last night, after a seriously hot make-out session and breathless agreement to continue where they'd left off when they'd have less of an audience for The Day After.

Partly because she was intensely curious what the creative connection between them would lead to in the bedroom, of course, especially added to what promised to be a fiery physical connection. But she had to admit she wondered whether he'd had this stunning ensemble hidden away in there, or if he'd managed to pick it up in town somewhere during the day.

Her efforts to play it cool were obviously failing miserably, or else Chris was doing his best to turn up the heat between them.

Every time their eyes met, he winked and flashed a flirty, confident smile that only pushed her curiosity and impatience to find out more closer to the red zone.

Thankfully, before she reached the end of her self-discipline and dragged him by his jacket's knotted belt into her apartment, the mysterious moment of eleven past the hour arrived.

Mrs. Seagon held up her glass that looked like a dark amethyst in the firelight and smiled at everyone one at a time.

"It's been such a joy having all of you here for this edition of Mid-Holiday Madness. I think everyone will agree our two-for-the-price-of-one bards have done a spectacular job with the stories this year."

She paused, beaming as everyone else cheered and applauded. Even BeeGirl joined in with a couple of soft barks and one long, drawn-out howl that set everyone to laughing.

For their part, EllaJane and Chris exchanged a secretive

smile, then both of them blushed at the applause and the hint of things to come.

"I trust everyone has figured out our mystery author?" Mr. Seagon said, his eyes twinkling as he waited for everyone to nod. "Then we're pleased to let you know we have a special event planned for the springtime, when she, EllaJane, and Chris will have a conversation about how it's been for them to work together. Assuming the two of you are willing, of course. It's certainly been a pleasure for me."

EllaJane let out a surprised laugh, once again turning to Chris. He grinned and scrubbed his fingers through his hair, but he was nodding.

"That sounds wonderful to me," EllaJane said. "Hopefully she'll feel we did her worlds proud."

"I'm quite certain she will," Mrs. Seagon said. "And just like the year will come to an end tomorrow night, so our nights of gathering to celebrate storytelling must as well. Thank you both, and we're in your very capable hands."

"Even though the secret is out, don't forget to take your books with you as you go." EllaJane waved one hand toward the beautiful tree still standing proud in the corner, with stacks of books underneath. "You might be surprised at what we picked out for you. Tonight's story is all about coming home, and about meeting your true family for the first time. I have to say that's been very much on my mind all week long."

The somehow...*inviting* look in Chris's eyes had EllaJane resisting the urge to grab his hand.

"There's a special magic to the family you find, whether those people are related to you or not. My Auntie June certainly found her most beloved place here at Odds and Endings, and I'm grateful to her every day for bringing me along. I'm sure she'd understand why I say experiencing it for myself has gone way past anything I could have imagined. And we're just getting started."

EllaJane had to take a breath to calm the cascading waves of excitement rampaging through her middle at that idea. So much more than her residency had begun here, especially this week.

And she couldn't wait to find out what would happen next.

"We're going not too terribly far from here," she finally said. "And only a few years into the future. We're visiting a world that's about to be transformed, and the people who will be in the middle of that storm on the horizon. But we'll see the beginning of what gives them a chance to find a new future together."

This time she was gratified to see Chris take his own deep, slow breath before she closed her eyes.

Letting herself drift away, to another magical town in the mountains.

To another beginning of a new life in the dead of winter.

EllaJane reached out for Chris and his steady supply of fuel, of energy to feed the fires of her imagination. The way he somehow brightened the path, and cleared the way for the story to come.

Walking in that imaginary playground with him by her side, EllaJane began to tell the tale.

DESPITE HIS MOSTLY UNREASONABLE paranoia about the mountains, Alex Collins fell in love with Wolf Branch, Virginia, at first sight.

Hs boyfriend Etan—who Alex had also fallen for the second they met—had overridden their car's autonav after long hours of letting it carry them southeast from Chicago. Then he'd used the rarely touched steering wheel to take them off the black ribbon of highway, along a scarily narrow gravel road, and out through thick stands of trees to a breathtaking stony overlook.

They now stood in the town's sheltering ring of mountains, rising up towering and gray to Alex's city-boy eyes, with the eerie music of thousands of tree branches bare for the winter chattering to each other.

But Wolf Branch itself sparkled and glowed even under the heavy afternoon clouds that greeted him on his first visit. Every bit as beautiful and welcoming as Etan had described it, both awake and in his frequent bouts of sleeptalking.

In the cozy bowl spread out below, the red brick buildings, neat grid of streets, and rainbow array of Christmas lights looked more like a movie set than a place where people lived. A rectangular town square right in the middle was outlined with streetlamps draped in wreaths glowing red and green, and Alex saw people and little stands and shelters gathered throughout.

All he could smell on the damp, snow-scented breeze was the trees and forest all around, but his stomach still growled at the sight of cooking fires at the holiday festival down below.

He had no doubt the breeze could kick up into a fierce wind from the blizzard stories Etan told. His tales of being snowed in for a month, more than once, had Alex alternating between fascinated and scared half to death.

Still, the air here felt almost soft. Gentle compared to the gales that blew in off Lake Michigan and howled through skyscrapers back in the city.

Etan leaned against the stubby hood of the car beside him, taking in the same view from an entirely different perspective, his delicate features and green eyes warm with what Alex guessed was the nostalgia of a native. He certainly looked the part, with a red and blue flannel shirt and jeans. Not all that different from what he wore to his university classes in Chicago, but it suited him better here in the land of his birth and childhood.

Alex had never been one to worry much about his own clothing, but he'd fallen victim to a stubborn case of meet-the-family nerves getting ready for this trip. No matter how many times Etan told him whatever he wore would be just fine, Alex had spent hours considering, coordinating, and eventually obsessing over what to pack.

For the big arrival, he'd settled on matching Etan as much as he could without being obvious enough to seem ridiculous. He knew the dark green sweater played up his red hair and beard, which he'd had trimmed for the occasion.

Comfortable enough for his engineering job, but nowhere near formal enough for a gathering with his own family. The fact that Alex had jumped at the chance to head south instead of north to Wisconsin for this holiday made his preferences more than clear enough.

Etan slipped his warm hand into Alex's.

"You doing okay? Or are you about to abandon me here and scoot back to Chicago?"

Alex laughed and shook his head.

"I couldn't get back even if I wanted to, you know that. All you'd have to do is use your phone to disable the autonav and I'd be stranded. The idea of trying to drive scares me a hell of a lot more than meeting your family."

Etan stared at him, one eyebrow raised, while the wintery breeze rippled his fine brown hair.

"You know, you might end up wishing you'd learned to drive after all by the time the Griffith clan is through with you."

Alex stared back, reasonably sure Etan was teasing him. He'd never ventured anywhere with what could properly be called hills, much less mountains. And he hated to admit—even to himself—that his lifetime in the Midwest and years in the city had given him an unease about this landscape.

A closed-in feeling that he couldn't *see* far enough, that anything in the world could be right around the corner and he'd have no idea until it was too late.

Combine that with his lack of knowledge about such a different culture and the feeling of wanting to impress the family of the man he'd fallen so hard in love with in an incredibly short time, and he wasn't fully confident about much of anything.

Except that letting himself get dragged out to a noisy party in the middle of a Chicago snowstorm, the reluctant decision that let him and Etan cross paths, had been the best decision of Alex's life.

Thank the gods a twitch at the corner of Etan's entirely kissable, smartass mouth gave the game away before Alex managed to get himself good and nervous.

Worse than he already was, anyway.

"Jackass," Alex said, pretending to push Etan away. "Do your parents know what a jerk you've turned into since you left home?"

Etan shrugged, but his grin broke through.

"Turned into? You'll find out over the next few days how very little I've changed. Come on, let's get on to Mom and Dad's house. I can hear your belly pitching a fit, and I promise they'll be waiting impatiently to stuff you silly."

Alex stood for a few more seconds, letting his eyes take in the town where Etan had grown up. The thick clouds had lowered enough that tendrils caressed the tops of the mountains, flowing across the highest points and wandering down toward Wolf Branch. Probably bringing that snow he smelled, and hopefully not enough to make the already twisting and challenging roads treacherous.

Even if the landscape spooked Alex, it had *shaped* Etan. Formed him. Same with his family, who Alex already knew were far more tight-knit than his own.

He hoped he'd be able to fit himself into a place so important to Etan, find a place within that family.

Without making a jackass of himself in the process.

MUCH AS HE enjoyed the unusual chance to drive in manual —putting the just-in-case lessons he'd stubbornly insisted on to use—Etan Griffith breathed a sigh of relief as he got back to the highway and re-engaged the autonav.

Even traveling a route he knew well enough to follow in his sleep, and often did, his trembling hands and jittery nerves turned a nice challenge into a bad idea.

He knew he should focus on the road anyway as the gray half-circle of the steering wheel folded itself back into the matching padded dashboard, while the pedals did the same disappearing act under his feet. The broad display above the dash informed him they'd be another eighteen minutes on the way to his parents' house in glowing blue letters.

He thought that calm, ordinary text should have been livened up to fit the occasion instead, to match the over-heated gyrations of excitement in his stomach, heart, and mind.

Displayed on the curve of the windshield, perhaps, where he played movies during long drives sometimes, or set it to dim for sleep or privacy. With the words backed up by multi-colored explosions and streamers and ribbons.

Sort of like fireworks, but with his own body supplying the *boom*.

The town square was packed full today, with one of the last days of the holiday festival in full swing. The tradition went back much further than his almost twenty years, giving everyone in Wolf Branch and within driving distance a chance to shop, socialize, and relax before the real craziness of the holiday week settled in.

Often before or after serious winter weather kept them all at home for days or weeks at a time.

Etan had fond memories of spending hours there as a kid, helping out with some school project or other, or more often working the fundraiser and educational booth for the cannery with his grandparents. The magic of preserving food, of seeing fruit and vegetables and even meat transformed, smelling the steamy air in the noisy cannery, and then enjoying the harvest months after it happened never lost its joy for him.

He'd thought about stopping for that as he had on this trip home before. Giving Alex a chance to experience warm sweet potato pie, savory hand pies, and extremely old-fashioned Appalachian candy made from honey and maple syrup and the thrifty imaginations of generations past.

The chance to grab their choice of hot drinks alone would be worth the time, with the option for hot cider made from the apples, cherries, pears, or blueberries grown all around Wolf Branch. A similar variety of beer and wine would be on hand as well, with harder spirits easy to get if you knew who to ask.

But Etan was afraid he'd only let himself get more worked up and eager if they waited, with every introduction before the big one leaving him more impatient to get home.

Because out of all the casual dates and quick flings of his years here and in Chicago, Alex was the first one Etan truly wanted his parents to like. Not in a needing-their-approval kind of way, though that would be a fantastic side benefit, of course.

This was because having the three people who *got* him,

who knew him best in the world, together in one room and falling in love with each other was Etan's idea of pure heaven.

The main thing he was worried about, besides the possibility of more snow than expected keeping them from heading back in a few days, was Alex being bored silly by the whole thing. That or deciding Etan really was a hopeless country boy after all no matter how well they'd been getting along so far.

"So your parents have enough to keep us fed if the snow really comes down?" Alex said, his blue eyes twinkling. "They probably aren't used to trying to keep up with a big, strapping Midwestern boy."

Etan snorted and leaned in for a coffee-scented kiss. Alex was several inches taller and much broader and more muscular, and he wasn't kidding about his eating abilities.

"You'd be surprised how folks cook back here in the mountains, especially when company is coming. They'll have enough to feed themselves, both of us, and at least five or six more. You'll eat 'til you're begging for mercy, sweetheart. I just hope you don't get antsy for bit of city life after a couple of days."

"I'll do my best to keep up at mealtimes, then. If they're going to keep me that well-fed, I doubt I'll be in any kind of a hurry to leave. This town makes a pretty big deal out of the holidays, huh? Looks like a land of make-believe to me, in the best possible way."

They'd passed the several cozy blocks of Wolf Branch by, with all the storefronts adorned with holiday cheer and full of lingering shoppers wanting to beat the storm. But all the houses scattered along the way out of town were equally strung up in lights and giant Santa figures, with decorated trees and stacks of massive presents.

"All the little towns around here have a contest every year, and we win pretty often. Our only real competition is

Bountyfield and Hidden Springs. A place way up in the mountains called Lightning Gap graciously bowed out a while back because they won constantly. No one kicked up a fuss when you were growing up?"

Alex smiled and wrinkled his nose.

"Sure, beautiful decorations and all, lights and boozy parties, the whole works. And my mother makes a painfully festive production out of every occasion, whether anyone wants her to or not, no matter how much my father complains. Something about the mountains all around, though, the way the town is kind of cradled here. Feels like..."

He paused, and his shy smile turned Etan's heart into a lovestruck puddle all over again.

And there it was, the same sense of an internal click. The powerful feel of some misaligned part of Etan slipping into the right rhythm at last. Like discovering how a piece of his life's puzzle was meant to fit after years of wondering.

Exactly how he'd felt they first time their eyes met.

"I don't know," Alex said, his voice soft, and strangely melancholy. "This sounds weird, even for me, but it feels like a *good* place. You're lucky to have this to come home to."

He looked out the window, toward a steep drop-off rolling hundreds of feet down to the Grasppe River and a set of old train tracks. Etan didn't have to see for himself to know the water would be choppy and gray this time of year, with stands of bare sycamore trees and their massive limbs sprawling along the ragged edges of marshy land.

One of the rare things Alex hesitated to talk about was his prickly relationship with his own family, rarely seen or heard from. But one of Etan's strangely deep hunches told him this was a time when *not* asking would be a mistake.

"Sure your folks are okay with this? You spending Christmas and New Year's down here, I mean?"

Alex let out a sigh big enough to fog the windshield for a second.

"Eh, you know. It's more like I'm leaving a checkbox unfilled than anything else. The trouble is my parents will have to explain where I am, and worse, *why* I'm not there lined up like a dutiful son. Pretty much the same game since I left home. But the truth is we'll all breathe a sigh of relief that we don't have to pretend to like each other. As long as I fall back into place before my father's usual huge birthday party, we'll pretend this never happened."

Etan let out his own much slower breath. Alex said it so casually, like he'd sounded talking about the traffic that morning, or when to stop for lunch.

His voice and face had been about a thousand times more animated when he explained in great and fascinating detail how the hundreds of gigantic windmills they'd seen along the drive functioned, from the spinning blades to the control pod way at the top to delivering electricity.

Etan hadn't paid much attention to them for most of his life, even though there was a huge bunch in Maple Ridge, bringing power to Wolf Branch for decades. But thanks to Alex, he understood them now, appreciated how they were made and what they did.

He wanted to understand that much about Alex, too.

"I'm guessing you won't be taking me home to meet them anytime soon, huh?"

Alex scowled and shook his head.

"No, it's not like that. They'd probably like you just fine. In fact I know they would, just nowhere near as much as *I* like you. We've never made sense to each other is all. It kind of amazes me how you and your parents stay in touch all the time, to tell you the truth. I wish I'd had the chance to meet your grandparents."

The car slowed right before the turn onto the much

smaller side road, away from the occasional house and business on the outskirts of Wolf Branch and into a vast sprawl of forest. The kind of place where people counted their home-places in acres rather than square feet.

Then on to the house where Etan had grown up, with his beloved grandparents not far away.

And, he hoped, to the chance for Alex to find the family he'd been missing.

"I wish you'd had a chance to meet them too. It's all going to be good, Alex. I'm glad you're here."

Alex took a slow, deep breath, then leaned his head against Etan's shoulder.

"Me too. I'll be on my best behavior, promise."

BY THE TIME the car turned itself up a long, twisting driveway, Alex's disorientation was getting uncomfortably profound. Turned out his rock-solid sense of direction and location failed utterly away from flat land, towering buildings, and grid-like streets.

The road out of Wolf Branch had twisted and turned, rose and fell, curving through mountains so close that he could barely see the darkening skies. He was afraid to watch the autonav's map instead. The threat of having to ask Etan to pull over so Alex could puke passed beyond uncomfortable and into horrifying.

For all he knew, they could be on any side of Wolf Branch, ten miles away or a hundred yards.

And still, Alex's other sense he'd relied on throughout his life carried on steady as his heartbeat.

He saw, he *felt* patterns all around him. In the way the trees grew close against the road, how their branches interlaced, letting the light through or hiding it. In the weather-flattened grass and weeds alongside the road. Even in the way the creek that had worn down this passage between the mountains shifted and flowed within its channel.

He'd seen the same thing drawing him out of Fond du Lac and toward Chicago, then pulling him toward that party the first night he and Etan met.

To see and feel the same thing now—showing him their convoluted path as surely as unseen satellites directed the car —gave him much-needed reassurance that he was right where he was supposed to be.

"There you go," Etan said with a smile. "The source of me and all my multi-faceted strangeness. Or at least where they did their best to keep me fed and watered."

Up ahead, a two-story house was tucked into a little valley, with the brown siding and green roof making it look like it had grown there. A broad porch wrapped around the front, and the neatly trimmed lawn was dotted with stone planters of all shapes and sizes. Not far behind the house, the hillside rose up close, with several splashes of evergreens breaking up the brown and gray.

No trace of the showy lights and figures from back in town, not out here. Only a row of long, color-changing icicles along the top of the porch and a huge, red-ribboned wreath on the wooden door. So much nicer than the cutthroat neighborhood holiday extravaganzas he'd been dragged around to ogle growing up.

"Your father built this place? It's beautiful."

"Well, he's a contractor, so he didn't do all of it himself. But he and Mom designed the whole thing, and Dad did a bunch of the work. He still constantly tinkers with it to this day."

The car slowed, aiming itself toward the silvery arc of charging station just to the left of the porch, just as the door opened. A woman with waves of curly blonde hair stepped out, followed immediately by a man with the same brown hair as Etan. They were both dressed in similar clothes as Alex, letting him shed his worry of standing out on that front.

"That's the true source of my strangeness," Etan said. The car stopped and shut itself down, the display switching to show all the stats from the trip. For once, Alex couldn't possibly care less about that. "Go on, I'll get the car hooked up. I'm sure they're about to bust with wanting to meet you."

The man and the woman had indeed made it from the porch to the car in a flash, and they now waited outside Alex's door. At the sight of their huge smiles, his protest about letting them say hello to Etan first died a slow and easy death.

He stepped out and into a laughing, two-for-one bearhug. A chorus of welcomes rang out directly into his ears.

"Alex, I'm so glad to finally meet you!"

"About time you two made it."

"Come on inside out of this cold."

"Both of you have got to be about half-starved."

He was laughing himself by the time they stepped back and gave Etan the same treatment.

Etan took his hand and gave it a good squeeze.

"Alex Collins, meet Laura and Connor Griffith. Mom and Dad, this is Alex. Not sure what it says about all of you that you have me in common, but you'll have to work that out for yourselves."

"You just leave all your stuff out here for now," Connor said, waving his hand toward the house. "We'll get it all later. Right now we've got enough roasted chicken, baked potatoes, and veggies ready to feed a small army."

"And a whole bunch of getting to know you to do," Laura said. "We might have a lot more time for that if these clouds deliver on their promise this evening, but we may as well get started. Welcome home."

The two of them headed toward the house, leaving Etan grinning at Alex, who laughed under his breath and shook his head.

"You ready for all this?" Etan said. "Not that you have a chance in hell of getting away now. Seems to me my parents and these mountains were just waiting all these years to welcome you."

Alex looked around again, at the sheltering valley, not as grand as the one around Wolf Branch but no less comforting. At the solid bulk of the house, brand new and somehow familiar.

At the first huge, impossibly light snowflakes drifting down, catching the warm light from inside the house. The light Etan had grown up by.

And at Etan himself: the first, best place Alex had ever found to truly be himself.

The person he most wanted beside him now and as far into the future as he could imagine.

Alex kissed him, quick and sweet.

"This might sound weird, even for me," he said, "but this really does feel like home."

Etan grabbed his hand, and the two of them walked toward their future.

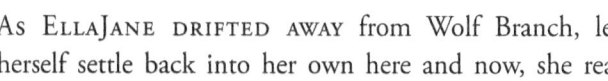

As EllaJane drifted away from Wolf Branch, letting herself settle back into her own here and now, she realized she'd taken on at least one vital element of the story in the world around her.

She still sat in the cozy basement of Odds and Endings, and she smelled the fire and the Christmas tree and the earthy sweetness of elderberry wine. She heard the sighs and then applause around her, and when she opened her eyes, she saw the riot of colors in everybody's clothing.

But her right hand was no longer folded with her left in her lap, or held flat along her thigh.

It was held warm and safe in Chris's hand, and she knew it had been for a while now.

When she looked into his eyes, he squeezed her hand and nodded, and that squeeze brought her all the way back into her utterly fantastic reality.

And the strangest part, or at least the part that surprised her, was the way no one at all acknowledged the change, the outward and public shift in their relationship. EllaJane had to fight back a giggle when she realized they'd likely been expecting this all along.

Probably a good bit more than she or Chris had.

The thousands of books and many millions of words around her shifted, turning themselves from ordinary black marks on paper into impressions of people and places. Lives as real as her own, from birth to love to passing away, all of them vibrant and rich and vivid enough to touch.

More than she ever had before, EllaJane found herself swept up in the peculiar joy and thrill and mystery of telling stories. The magic.

The thing she'd done for herself since she was old enough to grasp words and their meaning, and that she never stopped feeling incredibly lucky to be able to share.

Finding a group of people who understood her love for it, her passion, seemed as unlikely as the most far-fetched and fanciful tale in this whole grand house.

But the truth beamed and smiled all around her.

"That was just lovely, EllaJane," Venus said, her shimmering scarlet granny nightgown catching the light as she absently rubbed BeeGirl's head flopped comfortably in her lap. "One of my favorite things is hearing new stories about characters I know and love so much. Gives the whole thing... I don't know, a *settled* feeling, like the story world just keeps going on and the characters keep living their lives even when we're not watching. It's comforting somehow."

"So you know the mystery author for sure," EllaJane said. "Anyone else still wondering?"

Everyone smiled and shook their heads, with a look of satisfaction rather than disappointment. Exactly what Ella-Jane had been hoping for.

"Still looking forward to seeing what books you've got picked out for us," Kay said, sitting snuggled close up against Adam. The effect of their matching pajamas made them look like one fabulous pile of Christmas presents. "I'm going to guess you came up with some good ones."

"That we did," Chris said. He squeezed EllaJane's hand again and raised his eyebrows, asking more than one question without saying a word.

"Go ahead and spill the surprise," she said. "Seems fair since I got to tell one more story than you did."

He laughed, shaking his head and leaning closer to her, setting off sparkling warmth through her middle a lot like the glittering bits of fire heading toward the chimney. She was more determined than ever to find out where he'd gotten that delicious smoking jacket, and see him out of it.

"I'm an absolute beginner compared to anyone with a book on these shelves, and to you." He gestured toward the tree, still flickering with a dozen colors and patterns too varied and quick to predict. Their stacks of books waited underneath, with a single plain-paper-wrapped one in each bundle. "We didn't find the secret books on any of the shelves here, or anywhere else. We got our hands on a brand-new short story collection, one that's not even out to the general public yet. All of them set within series, too. The three of us decided that would be the perfect gift to go with our ventures into fan fiction."

The whole group exclaimed excitedly, sending BeeGirl's ears flying as her head popped up at the noise. Mrs. Seagon clasped her hands under her chin with a huge, delighted grin on her face, sending the shiny red noses on the group of girly reindeers on her sweatshirt sparkling.

"Oh, that *is* a wonderful surprise! We can spend our New Year's Eve curled up with a whole group of fantastic characters, courtesy of three of our favorite writers. I can't think of a better way to start a new year. Thank you both so much."

All of them stood, converging roughly in the middle of the cozy basement, and the flurry of hugs left EllaJane breathless. She made a point of kneeling so BeeGirl in her squirrel-covered nightgown could add her appreciation in a burst of sweet kisses.

Mr. and Mrs. Seagon stood hand in hand in front of the fireplace, their silvery hair turned red and gold by the fire-light. For a second, EllaJane saw them as so much younger rather than their current age that she could never guess (and would never ask).

They were middle-aged, solid and comfortable in them-selves and each other. They were in their twenties, starting out fresh and new and unsure, but confident and relying on the love they shared.

They were just kids, school-aged and awkward, not yet understanding the connection they felt. Facing decades of change they couldn't imagine, years of happiness and joy, tragedy and sadness. And somehow already drawn toward the path they would share for so wonderfully long.

EllaJane turned to Chris with a gasp on her lips, and knew from the dazed look in his eyes that he'd seen it too.

They both jumped when Mr. Seagon spoke. The twinkle

in his eyes made it clear he hadn't missed their startled response.

"Much like watching the year pass, closing our week of enjoying storytelling right out loud brings both melancholy and happiness. Giving us a chance to hear the words as the writer conjured them, and share each other's company. To look forward and behind us, and appreciate what's been and what's to come. And one of the best parts about printed stories is we can revisit them and recapture a bit of that magic. I hope you'll both be willing to set your words to paper so we can do just that."

A shiver rippled along EllaJane's spine at the idea of her own stories finding space on these shelves alongside so many who'd gone before. She'd known that would happen since she found out she'd gotten the year-long residency. Looked forward to it. But she hadn't understood what it would really mean to her until that moment.

How far into the future would people be visiting this enchanted place, searching and finding the trace of herself and Chris left behind?

The ordinary and extraordinary idea brought tears to her eyes.

"Of course," Chris said, and she heard the emotion in his voice as well. "I mean, I can only speak for myself."

"We both will," EllaJane said. She stepped back to his side and reclaimed his hand, warm and solid in her own. "Having something to share and to remember this week by sounds fantastic to me."

"We'll look forward to that," Mrs. Seagon said with her own sparkling eyes and knowing smile. "And we'll leave the two of you with our gratitude, and our warmest wishes that you treasure the memories of our Mid-Winter Madness. And everything that found its beginning here."

Ivy walked up to EllaJane, holding a big, clear canning

jar full of her so-purple-it-was-nearly-black "wine." The effect of that combined with her ruffly pink granny gown and a decidedly wicked smile had EllaJane returning the grin.

"We always make a point of giving our Mid-Holiday Madness Bard a start on their New Year's Eve celebrations, as a small thank you for sharing your storytelling. If you'd rather have some of the Seagons' good bourbon, that's fine, too. Either way, I reckon we've got enough for both of you."

Chris glanced at EllaJane, and she knew they were on the same side of this decision between two wonderful things. It seemed the connection they forged while writing together worked in real life, too.

"Well, *I* think the choice is obvious," he said. "But I'll defer to EllaJane's good judgement."

"In that case, I'll simply say thank you very much, Ivy. And this will get the new year off to an excellent start."

Ivy handed the jar over, gave both Chris and EllaJane an assessing gaze, then snorted and shook her head.

"Seems to me you two got pretty much everything you're going to need for tonight, tomorrow night, and however long into the future you decide to take it. See you in the new year."

She joined Venus and BeeGirl, and they all walked up the stairs together, following Kay and Adam. Only the Seagons waited, hand in hand much like EllaJane and Chris.

"I get the very strong feeling you understand your true gift of the week," Mrs. Seagon said. "But we always want to make sure."

"Something changed," EllaJane said, waiting for Chris to nod before she went on. "I felt and I even *saw* the books and the stories come to life. Like something about tonight let me cross a line, maybe. One I can't say I understand, but it feels wonderful."

Mr. Seagon nodded. "That's the magic of Odds and

Endings. You're part of it now, and it's part of both of you. Every writer and character and lover of stories who spends time here make it richer and stronger. It's been that way since the first tales were shared in this basement a long time ago. Having both of you telling stories now is sure to take everything to fantastic new heights. We're all lucky to have you here, and thank you."

EllaJane and Chris said "We're the lucky ones" in perfect unison.

Mrs. Seagon leaned her head against Mr. Seagon's shoulder and nodded.

"You certainly are. Good night."

Once they made their way up the stairs, taking the last two bundles of books with them, EllaJane turned to Chris.

"I've got a lot of things in mind for the rest of the night, and hopefully a hell of a lot longer than that. But first things first. Where on *earth* did you get that amazing jacket?"

He smiled, and his eyes shone brighter than the fire.

"Would you believe it was here already? When I got back here this afternoon, I asked Mr. Seagon if he knew where I could pick up something fun for tonight, to liven up my rather monochromatic wardrobe. He held up one finger and nearly ran toward the back of the bookstore. I swear I heard him giggling all the way back out front, and he presented me with this groovy ensemble. I have to say you're looking pretty damn hot yourself."

EllaJane put the jar of precious liquid on one of the little antique tables and stepped closer.

"You're into cartoon characters, huh?"

He laughed under his breath and captured her other hand.

"I'm into someone who's confident enough wear a nightshirt covered with them, and cool enough to go with the old-school ones. Truth is, EllaJane, I'm just into you."

She leaned into his almost delicate kiss, and now she felt the combined heat and passion of tens of thousands of love stories in the basement and throughout Odds and Endings.

Most of all the hopeful beginning for Susan and Paul waiting for the Santa Train, Beth and Mark sharing their first holiday and realizing the extent of their combined magic, and Alex discovering his true home, family, and future with Etan.

"Wow," he whispered against her lips. "I can't be the only one who's feeling all of that...*everything*."

She shook her head, not moving away. All the nerves in her body tingled and fired.

"You're not. We've got a hell of a night and a whole lot more in front of us, Chris. I say it's high time we got started."

ABOUT KARI

Kari Kilgore's wanderlust and imagination lead her all over the world on grand adventures. Her heart and family bring her home to her native Appalachian Mountains of Virginia. From that solid base, she and her husband Jason A. Adams bring those adventures to life in fiction.

Time to read (and write) stories of all kinds brings joy to her winter holidays.

Kari writes fantasy, mystery, romance, science fiction, and contemporary fiction, and she's happiest when she surprises herself. She lives at the end of a long dirt road in the middle of the woods with Jason, various house critters, and wildlife they're better off not knowing more about.

The Confidential Adventure Club

For Kari's exclusive free After The End stories and deleted scenes, discounts, early pre-sale releases, adorable pet photos, and a whole lot more not available anywhere else, join us in The Club.

Hope to see you there!

www.KariKilgore.com
www.SpiralPublishing.net
www.ConfidentialAdventureClub.com

bookbub.com/authors/kari-kilgore

amazon.com/author/karikilgore

goodreads.com/karikilgore

facebook.com/kari.kilgore.1

ALSO BY KARI KILGORE

I hope you enjoyed reading the stories in *A Tapestry of Holiday Tales* as much as I enjoyed writing them.

Ready to spend more time in Lightning Gap and the magical Odds and Endings bookstore? The secret door awaits at www.KariKilgore.com/LightningGap.

You'll find the path to the ever-expanding world of Arch Knight and Misfortune and Magic at www.KariKilgore.com/MisfortuneAndMagic.

Catch up with Jean, Father Hall, and the rest of The Odd Society by visiting www.KariKilgore.com/TheOddSociety.

Discover how Mark and Beth (and Janie) met and more by swinging by www.KariKilgore.com/VoicesThroughTime.

The world of Storms of Future Past and more with Alex and Etan awaits at www.KariKilgore.com/StormsofFuturePast.

If you're craving more adventures from the Appalachian Mountains, and in many genres, head over to www.KariKilgore.com/TalesFromAppalachia.

For more fantasy of many kinds, visit www.KariKilgore.com/Fantasy. If you're in a romantic mood, you'll find more at www.KariKilgore.com/Romance.

Be the first to know about release dates and check out more of my fiction, including almost every genre, at www.KariKilgore.com.

The Storms of Future Past Series:

Dreaming the Storm

Joining the Storm

Into the Storm

Fighting the Storm

Sensing the Storm: A Storms of Future Past Prequel

Storms of the Heart: A Storms of Future Past Romance

Storms of Future Past Books One through Four Collection

The Odd Society:

Independent by Means of Magic

Protected by Means of Magic

The Voices through Time Series:

Songs in the Mountain

Secrets in the Land

Walking the Ghosts: A Voices through Time Novella

Dispatches from the Galaxy Stories:

Restricted Species

The Becalmed

The Garbage Belt

Plurapod Pathogen

The Changes Cascade

Novels:

Until Death

The Dream Thief

Hand Me Downs

Protecting Her Own

Novellas:

Legacy of the Land

In the Pines

DNA Never Lies

The Box of Possibilities

Collections:

Fantastic Women: A Dark Fantasy Novella Trio

Fantastic Shorts: Volume 1

Near Future Forward (with Jason A. Adams)

Fantastic Shorts: Volume 2

Partners in Romance (with Jason A. Adams)

Dispatches from the Galaxy: A Space Opera Novella Trio

Fantastic Shorts: Volume 3

Escape into Romance: A Collection of Sweet Beginnings

Stepping Out of Reality: Short Spells of Appalachian Magic

Facing Down Extraordinary: A Series of Ordinary Heroes

Hacking Cybercrime: Dana Sanderson Short Mysteries

Shadows Mountain Deep (with Jason A. Adams)

Investigations Beyond Belief: The Initial Adventures of Deb Powers: Otherworldly PI

Passages in the Real World: Six Stories of Life's Transitions

Fantastic Side Trips: Side Characters Take Center Stage

A Kaleidoscope of Cat Tales: Five Stories of Cats and People Who Love Them

ADDITIONAL COPYRIGHT INFORMATION